Understanding Art

A Reference Guide to Painting, Sculpture, and Architecture
in the Romanesque, Gothic, Renaissance, and Baroque Periods

Volume 2

SHARPE REFERENCE
ARMONK, NEW YORK

FITZROY DEARBORN PUBLISHERS
LONDON

SHARPE REFERENCE

Sharpe Reference is an imprint of M.E. Sharpe, Inc.
M.E. Sharpe, Inc.
80 Business Park Drive
Armonk, NY 10504

FITZROY DEARBORN PUBLISHERS
11 Rathbone Place
London W1P 1DE
England

Library of Congress Cataloging-in-Publication Data

Arte come riconoscere. English
Understanding art: a reference guide to painting, sculpture,
and architecture in the Romanesque, Gothic, Renaissance, and
Baroque periods.
p. cm.
Includes bibliographical references and index.
ISBN 0-7656-8024-6 (alk. paper)
1. Art, Medieval. 2. Art, Renaissance. 3. Art, Baroque.
N5940.A7813 1999
709'.2--dc21
99-15944
CIP

Cataloging-in-Publication Data is also available from the British Library

Printed and bound in Italy

The paper used in this publication meets the minimum requirements of American National
Standard for Information Sciences – Permanence of Paper for Printed Library Materials,
ANSI Z 39.48-1984

Italian text preparation supervised by:
Flavio Conti (Romanesque, Renaissance, Baroque)
Maria Cristina Gozzoli (Gothic)
Drawings: Mariarosa Conti, Fulvio Cocchi, Franco Testa
Translation: Erica and Arthur Propper (Gothic Art), Barbara Fisher (Romanesque)
Sharpe Reference art editor: Esther Clark
Fitzroy Dearborn art editor: Delia Gaze
Cover design by Lee Goldstein

Contents

Renaissance Art

The artistic movement known as the Renaissance was born in Florence, Italy, in the first decades of the 15th century. By the end of this century its influence had spread all over the Italian peninsula. The movement's greatest achievements date from the first half of the 16th century, when Rome came to replace Florence as the leading center of artistic activity. It was during this period that its influence began to spread throughout Europe, starting a total artistic revolution, the effects of which continued to be felt almost to the present day. Although internally complex and varied, this movement elaborated original and typical but fairly consistent artistic principles, methods and forms. The object of this chapter is to describe and analyze typical works produced in Italy and elsewhere between the early 15th and mid-16th centuries.

Opposite page
Raphael, The Marriage of the Virgin, *1504; Milan, Pinacoteca di Brera.*

The Renaissance style derived its influence from two main sources. The first was a return to the characteristic forms of classical Greek and Roman art, after an interval of almost a millennium. The second was the application of the newly discovered technique of perspective, which enabled the artist to reproduce spatial depth on paper (or any other flat surface) with scientific accuracy. The former element was of particular interest to architects, for unlike the painters of the time, they could draw inspiration from the monuments of classical antiquity still in existence. The very name of the new movement, – Renaissance or rebirth – declared this influence. Those who proposed it considered themselves heirs to the tradition of classical art and consciously sought the "rebirth" of its forms or, at least, its spirit. They totally rejected the artistic achievements that had succeeded those of Greece and Rome, moved partly by their admiration of classical art but mainly by a deep-rooted conviction that art, like science, has its own laws and that these had been discovered and applied by the artists of the ancient world. Perspective, the second element, was merely the most striking of a number of revolutionary discoveries (oil painting, the preparation of frescos using cartoons, the rediscovery of the equestrian statue, the use of *stiacciato* in relief, the introduction of metal ties and so on). It was a decisive element in the development of the new art because it enabled the artist to provide a realistic sketch – a scheme that made clear to everyone what a proposed work would look like when finished. Indeed the idea emerged that the design was the most essential aspect of any work of art. This opened the way for the artist's passage from the ranks of the craftsman to the status of an intellectual. Previously it had been the corporation (the medieval guild) that counted. Since the Renaissance, however, the history of art has been dominated by the stories of individual artists. Recognizing Renaissance art means, above all, identifying the styles of the individual artists: Brunelleschi, Leon Battista Alberti, Masaccio, Raphael, Michelangelo, and so on. This conception of art as personal achievement still applies today.

Many other Renaissance concepts, attitudes and terms are still in use. The meaning given to the word "art;" the division of art into fine (in the form of architecture, sculpture, and painting), minor, and applied arts; the distinction between

Filippo Brunelleschi, The doorway of the Ospedale degli Innocenti (Foundling Hospital) in Florence. The features that were to become typical of 15th-century architecture are already visible in this first example: the return to a concept of architectural order, round-headed arches, a simple general plan and the subordinate role played by sculpture, which was limited to specific areas.

the architect, responsible for the form of a building, and the engineer, who guarantees its technical aspects; the deep-rooted conviction that a painting or a statue must "reproduce" something; and the even more resolute idea that there is a mathematical rule that separates the "beautiful" from the "ugly" all originated during the Renaissance. A study of the most characteristic and significant forms of Renaissance art must not merely trace the causes from which these forms developed but also those that have made our civilization what it is.

Architecture

History is made by individuals; that was the Renaissance view. And at least as far as architecture is concerned it is right. Renaissance architecture was created in Florence in the 1420s by one brilliant and obstinate man, Filippo Brunelleschi. Although the creation of this style was of an individual nature it had a collective value. Its forms were based on a number of rules that were open to rational examination and improvement, a common language.

This style was based on a fundamental decision made by Brunelleschi and confirmed by all his successors. This was the decision to use the forms of classical architecture in their buildings. In particular, they favored those adopted by the ancient Romans, mainly because they were better known and seemed more advanced and impressive than the Greek ones. The reasons behind this decision were numerous and complex and included what would today be called chauvinistic ones. The Italians, and the Florentines in particular, irritated by the pretensions of the German emperors, considered themselves sons and heirs of ancient Rome and its traditions. Basically, however, Brunelleschi was brought to this decision by purely technical

considerations. He held that architecture based on classical principles was more likely to be consistent with the ideals being developed in the new century than the Gothic style then in vogue. The vision of a world based on faith was, in the 15th century, being replaced by one based on reason. And reason, or rather rationality, was the very foundation of classical architecture, the forms of which were grouped according to fixed patterns. Every architect had at his disposal a system of standard solutions to most problems. He was thus free to focus his attention on the new

problems posed by his task. The first advantage of this system was the great savings of time and effort. The second was the opportunity for constant improvement. Every architect started from a common rule and came up with his own interpretation on the basis of the case at hand. Those who followed him could carry on from where he had left off, discarding the negative elements and adopting the positive solutions. In time they achieved almost total perfection. Just such a method had created the supreme grace of the Parthenon. The Greeks had in fact invented the process.

Starting from the temple, their most characteristic building type, and the technique of placing blocks of stone on top of one another, they had established standard forms for columns and entablatures, focusing attention on the relationships between these shapes to establish what was called an architectural order. The Romans had adopted this system in full but as they cultivated a type of architecture based on concrete vaults and not blocks of stone, it had been limited to the decoration of facades. To the three orders – Doric, Ionic, and Corinthian – they had

The fundamental principle: architectural order

Filippo Brunelleschi, who initiated Renaissance architecture, based the new language on the idea – conceived by the Greeks and used after them by the Romans – of "architectural order," the body of rules of form and proportion that bind all the parts of a building together in a set manner.

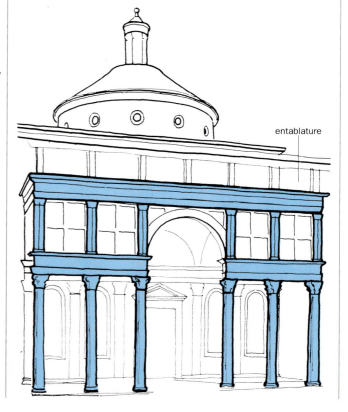

entablature

Filippo Brunelleschi, the Pazzi Chapel, outside the church of Santa Croce in Florence. Built between 1430 and 1444, this is one of the peaks of 15th-century architecture. In the 16th century the motif of the façade, with side colonnades joined by an entablature and a central arch, was given the name "serliana" (after Sebastiano Serlio).

Façades: the palace

The palace, the city residence of the rich merchant or nobleman, is a type of construction that was established in the Renaissance and spread over most of Italy.

The façade of Palazzo Rucellai is one of the first to be articulated by tiered orders, that is a different architectural order used on each floor of the construction (Doric on the ground floor, Ionic on the first, Corinthian on the second). In the Palazzo Farnese this solution was applied only to the windows.

Right
The façade of Palazzo Rucellai in Florence, built by Leon Battista Alberti between 1447 and 1451.

Bottom
The façade of Palazzo Farnese in Rome, by Antonio da Sangallo the Younger and Michelangelo Buonarroti, dating from the first half of the 16th century.

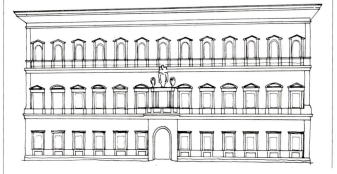

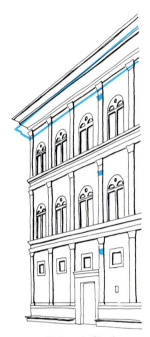

Lorenzo Ghiberti (?), the sacristy of Santa Trinità (Strozzi chapel), Florence. Palla Strozzi asked Ghiberti and his workshop to rearrange the architecture and sculptural decorations in the family chapel. Gray pietra serena *was used and enriched with decorative motifs (acanthus leaves abounding with animals) of late Classical derivation. Known mainly as a sculptor, Ghiberti was principally concerned with bronze casting and is famous for two doors on the Florentine Baptistery, his life's work. In Florence he set up a workshop of bronze casters and taught an entire generation this difficult technique. His pupils include painters and sculptors who were later to become famous, such as Donatello, Masolino da Panicale, Paolo Uccello, and Michelozzo.*

added two more – the Tuscan (a simplified variation of Doric) and the Composite (an enriched variation of Corinthian). Brunelleschi had the opportunity to study Roman monuments in depth, then more numerous and better preserved than today. He quickly discovered their advantages and once back in Florence he decided to apply them, although there were many almost insurmountable difficulties. How he – and the architects who followed him – resolved these provides the best means of identifying

Façades : the church

The façade of Santa Maria Novella in Florence was completed by Leon Battista Alberti, who attempted to give a Renaissance appearance to the typical façade of a church with a tall and narrow nave. The use of two tiers of orders connected by two large scrolls later became almost standard. Alberti built Sant'Andrea

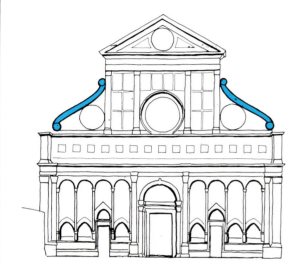

in Mantua entirely and created a second, far more original model for a façade, which was also to become successful. This was the "Giant" order (two stories high); it takes over the entire façade, and a smaller order repeats the proportions of the interior, creating a subdivision. The church was built in or around 1470.

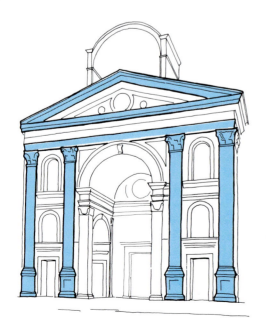

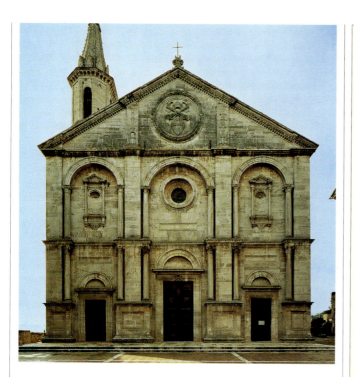

*Bernardo Rossellino, Pienza
cathedral, 1459-1462.*

and, at the same time, understanding of the new style. As has been seen, it was based mainly on "standard" forms. It was no longer necessary to work out the shape of each support and capital and the various parts of the decoration separately. Instead, it was sufficient to select one of the five orders and establish the proportions. The entire decorative scheme followed as a matter of course. The only remaining variable was the shape and size of the plan – decisions that were made by one man, the architect. The "creative" part of the work was entirely in his hands and the sculptors, decorators, painters,

glassmakers and other craftsmen just carried out his instructions. Medieval architecture had been based on a completely different system; architecture was not based on a unitary system of forms but on the invention of individual artists, restricted simply by tradition. The huge variety of choices to be made at all levels left room for the personal invention of each worker. The workers could not be expected to accept this downgrading willingly and indeed one of Brunelleschi's first works, the cupola of the cathedral in Florence, was troubled by an indefinite strike, to which the architect

THE OLD SACRISTY OF SAN LORENZO

Asked around 1410 to renew the old church of San Lorenzo (see photograph), Brunelleschi himself actually only completed the sacristy building, which was finished in 1428. This building has one cubic room, covered with a lower umbrella-dome sustained by pendentives – spherical triangles projecting from the corners of the walls. The adjacent presbytery repeats the model on a smaller scale, but with niches, which create gentle effects of chiaroscuro and expand the surfaces. The walls are marked by articulating elements (Corinthian pilasters strips, arches window frames) in *pietra serena* that trace the flat projection of the solids of which the construction is formed against the wall. Despite the contrasting spaces, the unitary nature of the whole is accentuated by the use of a single order, an entablature running unbroken through both spaces and the diffuse lighting. The only difference lies in the entrance to the presbytery. Here the columns and arches are doubled and the walls between the pilasters contain two doors with tympana crowned by shallow niches, bringing extra rhythm and plasticity. The decorations stand out against this framework. The architectural sculpture (capitals, frieze with cherubs) is extremely restrained. The sculptures attributed to Donatello and probably Michelozzo are richer: the bronze doors, the two saints in the niches, the medallions in the pendentives and at the top of the lunettes, all in stucco work or polychrome terracotta. Quite rightly, this building is considered a model of linear elegance and pure geometry, a crucial point in Brunelleschi's career because it contains the seed of elements that would be developed in later works. It was subsequently very influential outside Tuscany both for the clear and functional plan (copied mainly for mausolea and chapels) and for the visible achievement of a harmonious and ideal form defined by mathematical laws.

responded by firing the strikers without notice. The only way to overcome this difficulty was for the architect to see his authority recognized by those who commissioned the work. This was the path chosen by Renaissance architects with the result that Renaissance architecture remained an exclusively upper-class product, a "hothouse plant," as has rightly been said. Rarely is it to be seen outside the large cities and almost invariably in grandiose projects such as churches, palaces, and villas.

The second point is that the new movement took no interest in the structure of a building. It was concerned only

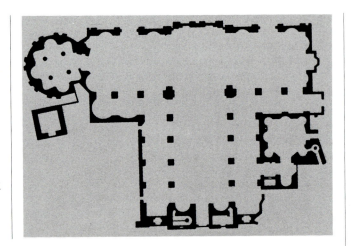

Donato Bramante, the mock choir of Santa Maria presso San Satiro, Milan. Perspective, that is the technique of scientifically reproducing the appearance of reality on a flat surface, was perhaps the most exciting discovery of the Renaissance. Here the choir could not be built behind the altar because of a street running behind the church, but is perfectly simulated by a trick of perspective.

Opposite page
Church of Santa Maria delle Grazie in Milan: the lantern and the gallery.

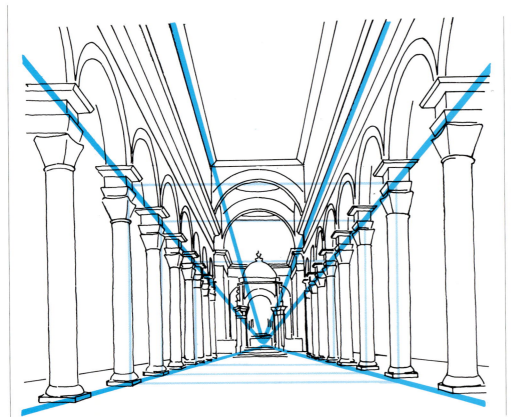

Interiors: perspective space
The interiors of churches also responded to the new criteria of perspective. They not longer featured a succession of independent bays but the walls were organized according to the architectural order, the dominant horizontal lines of which converged on a single point.

Below
Courtyard of the Palazzo Ducale in Urbino.

with the final appearance. This brought two consequences: on the one hand, an architecture that was far more "designed" than "constructed," and, on the other, the forsaking of all structural experimentation. The outcome was a new conception by which every building consisted of two parts: a masonry "box" that provided the framework and, superimposed on this, a decoration or "skin." The two parts could thus be designed separately. In other words, once he had established the shape and dimensions of a building, the

Renaissance architect could choose the order to be adopted and determine details and proportions. He could then proceed to "encase" the walls in the geometric pattern created by the building's columns and entablature. The box was important not in itself but as a support for the architectural orders. Before long, the building was being turned into a single coherent "theorem," and its functional aspects underestimated.

The box had to be given the casing that best suited the decoration. This – albeit in extremely schematic terms – is an outline of the entire system of Renaissance architecture, the mosaic formed by the piecing together of various buildings by different architects.

We can now examine the shapes adopted by this architecture. The stone box had to meet two requirements: since it was not the principal element, its construction had to require minimal efforts and it had to be built in such a way as to make the geometrical and mathematical content of the new art immediately apparent. Simple geometrical shapes such as cubes and parallelepipeds were

Brunelleschi, interior of the church of Santo Spirito, Florence.
The church is apparently designed on medieval models: a Latin cross plan, three aisles, and a central dome. However, nothing separates one bay from another and the unbroken friezes above the arches emphasize the fact that all the horizontal lines converge on a single point, using perspective.

therefore used. The proportions of height, width and depth were equally straightforward and easily perceived. Structures were also simplified. As supports for the roof, barrel and domical vaults were preferred to rib vaults, which are visually and structurally more complicated. Wherever possible vaults were replaced with wooden roofs that could be sustained by walls that were lighter, cheaper and easier to build. Alternatively, metal ties were inserted systematically between one vault and another to contain the thrust. Not only does the vault press its support downwards, it also tends to turn it outwards.

To overcome this problem the support must be reinforced or the outward thrust eliminated. The braces are visible but this does not matter; and they are "excluded" from the question of aesthetics, being considered "technical" aspects to be ignored by the eye. The pointed arch was banished completely and the only type to find favor was the semicircular arch. This alone was considered totally "rational" because its shape and

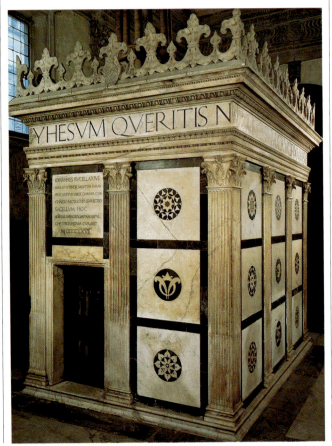

Left
Leon Battista Alberti, shrine of the Holy Sepulchre; Florence, San Pancrazio. An imaginary reconstruction, this work presents a strictly classical structure comprising surfaces adorned with geometric inlays in dimensions based on the golden section. The adoption of an internal organizational rule shows a desire for works to embody meanings that transcend their mere appearance. For Alberti these pure geometric decorations stimulate reflection on the truths of the faith.

Above
Staircase of the Laurenziana Library, designed by Michelangelo and completed by Bartolomeo Ammanati.

Opposite page
Michelangelo, Laurenziana Library, the reading room; Florence.
With a system of buttresses applied to the external walls in line with the slender pilasters on the inside, the masonry could be lightened and numerous windows inserted to light the interior. In the absence of aisles, a longitudinal division of the room into three is suggested by divisions on the wooden ceilings and the floor. A delicate rhythm is introduced by the pietra serena frames, enhanced by the warm colors of the wood and terra-cotta floor tiles.

size depend on a single factor, its radius, which could easily be linked geometrically with the rest of the building. Basically, this was a drastic and absolute simplification of all constructional aspects. For the decoration of this box or rather the form it was to have when finished, Renaissance architects turned to the classical orders. The 15th century saw the almost exclusive application of the two richest orders, the Corinthian and the Composite, distinguished by the characteristic, elaborate capital with carved acanthus leaves, a plant decoration distinctive of Mediterranean art. This was, however, used without adherence to the proportions fixed in antiquity, and variations were introduced to suit

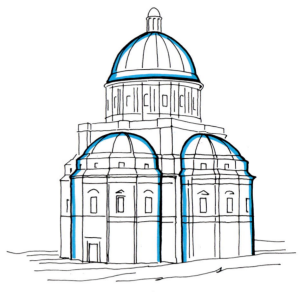

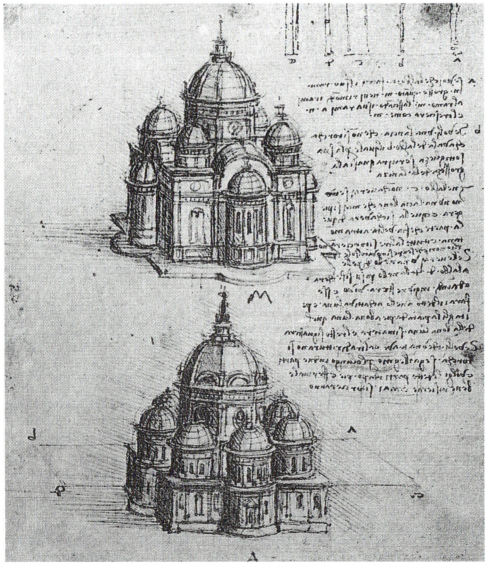

The ideal: total symmetry
Renaissance architecture was based on rational principles to which all was subordinate. As a result, all the axes – horizontal and vertical – of the ideal building were symmetrical, a characteristic form that started to appear during the late 15th and the early 16th centuries.

Left
Leonardo da Vinci, sketch of a church on a central plan; Paris, Institut de France.

162

Cola da Caprarola, church of the Consolazione, Todi. This building, by a minor artist recorded between 1494 and 1518, was completed at the beginning of the 17th century and illustrates a characteristic Renaissance theme, a building with a central plan, totally symmetrical around a single point.

Bottom
Giuliano da Sangallo, church of Santa Maria delle Carceri in Prato. Here a dome has been placed at the intersection of the arms of the cross to crown the building, completing its simple and elegant structure. The external facing of polychrome marble and reflects a tradition that had been common for centuries in Tuscan architecture.

different needs, usually with more slender shapes. Sixteenth-century practice adhered more rigorously to classical models but allowed greater freedom of choice. Such was the interest in their correct use that the architects of the times were the first to produce treatises that set forth a precise theory of the architectural orders (and sometimes, though less often, to apply this to their works). Since then this theory has been meticulously studied in every school of architecture.

They also added a third element to the two early ones (column and entablature), the pedestal, in turn divided into three parts. The proportions of the main parts were established: the height of the entablature was to be equal to a quarter of that of the column, that of the pedestal to a third. They also fixed a unit of measurement (the module) for each order; from then on all the measurements of an order could be expressed as multiples or submultiples of the module. This was the philosophy and language of the new style. We must now see the types of work produced with these criteria.

The main purpose of medieval architecture, had been the building of churches. That of the Renaissance added another in the form of palaces, built usually for the rich merchants that were appearing on the scene. In both churches and palaces the main problem was to determine the building's functional organization and design its façades. In palace architecture the first part of the problem was almost immediately resolved by placing four blocks around a central courtyard, forming a cube with a hollow center. This represented the best compromise between the desire for privacy (assured by the fact that all the rooms were connected by a loggia, or porticoed corridor, that opened

Left
Palazzo Ducale in Urbino: the Torricini façade.
The transformation of the old Urbino fortress into a Renaissance palace at the wish of Federico di Montefeltro was implemented in several stages. The main extension and organization of the palace were mostly built by Luciano Laurana, between 1465 and 1472, continued after this by Francesco di Giorgio Martini and not completed until 1534 by Cristoforo Genga. Laurana brilliantly resolved the numerous problems posed by an irregular plan, the presence of existing structures and great differences in the levels of the terrain, creating a harmonious whole with large rooms, a huge central courtyard, and broad facades.

Opposite page
Piazza del Campidoglio, Rome.
Designed by Michelangelo from about 1537 on as the center of city life, this square was completed over a long period of time (Palazzo Nuovo dates from the 17th century, the paving from 1940). The focal point is the statue of Marcus Aurelius (above), or rather its base with rounded corners, from which Michelangelo commenced the oval motif for the paving. This maintains the axis of the square and the centrality of the equestrian statue.

onto the courtyard) and the wish to be seen, satisfied by an imposing façade overlooking the street.

The façades to be embellished therefore were those overlooking the courtyard and that/those on the street. The former inevitably included a loggia. This was in the form of one or more rows of arches on columns or – as very quickly happened – the upper loggia was transformed into a gallery or closed corridor. A row of arches at ground floor level was topped with a number of windows (in line with the arches, centered above their apices) on the first floor and sometimes another row above.

An entablature in the same order as the

The dominant feature: the dome

Filippo Brunelleschi, dome of Santa Maria del Fiore, Florence.

The cupola is the dominant feature of nearly all Renaissance churches. The inspiration for this example was Roman and comes from the great dome of the Pantheon in Rome. The execution was, however, extremely different both in constructional technique (a double shell of bricks instead of a single block of concrete, see picture above) and in form. Characteristic features are the ribs and half-arches used to divide the various cells of the construction.

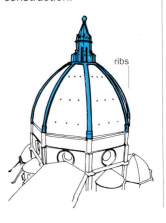

ribs

columns usually ran between the floors; a number of pilasters – the piers partially sunken in the wall – were placed on the upper floors in line with the floor columns of the ground. The façade on the street was more complicated to organise and the Renaissance developed not one but three models in succession. The first, called

rustication, was used by Brunelleschi himself; this was a great success throughout most of the 15th century and consisted in a wall covering of roughly squared stones. This covering – or facing to use the correct term – is used all over the façade broken only by the windows and a narrow decorated cornice between the floors. The

Michelangelo Buonarroti, dome of St. Peter's, Rome. Ribs are present once more, twice as many as at Santa Maria del Fiore. They are no longer single elements but connect the drum (the cylindrical part that supports the cupola) with columns and windows to the lantern (the element resembling a drum but smaller and placed on top of the dome). In this example, produced at the end of the Renaissance period (Brunelleschi's was at the very beginning), the "superimposed" dome of the early style has, a hundred and fifty years later, become "integrated" with the whole.

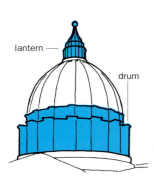

lantern

drum

unevenness and texture of the stone blocks usually improves from floor to floor and those on the top floor are sometimes perfectly smooth. Although much used in the 15th century, this finish was clearly not consistent with the principles of Renaissance architecture; it was regular and rational but too individual and its parts lacked a clear geometric imprint. As a result, a second type featuring different orders one above the other was soon developed. It is perhaps no accident that the first experiment in this style was undertaken by Leon Battista Alberti, the

Right
Palazzo Piccolomini in Pienza.

Below
Novella di Sanlucano, Palazzo Sanseverino (today the church of Gesù Nuovo) in Naples.
Despite a regular and well-proportioned plan, this external diamond-pointed facing is the result of Spanish influence – an indication of the cultural isolation of the outlying regions of the Aragonese kingdom from the other Italian states. Today little more than the external shell remains of the original construction, as in 1584 the palace was demolished and converted into the church of Gesù Nuovo.

second great architect of the 15th century and the first to write a treatise on architecture and to reflect upon the theoretical aspects of his work. This new style of façade was still rusticated but the windows were separated by as many pilasters and each floor corresponded to a particular order: from Tuscan on the ground floor, where the facing was roughest, up to Composite on the top. The floors were no longer separated by a simple cornice but by entablatures corresponding to the order of the columns supporting them. The whole building was practically enclosed in a mesh based on the

A revival: the villa
Renaissance Italy rediscovered a building type that had disappeared from Europe after the fall of the Roman Empire – the villa, the country residence of nobles and the wealthy. Reasons for its renewed popularity include the exercise of political power no longer by the single individual but by the state, from then on solely responsible for the construction of strongholds, and a safer countryside.

Andrea Palladio and Vincenzo Scamozzi, Villa Capra, known as "La Rotonda," Vicenza. Designed around the middle of the 16th century, this contains features typical of the Renaissance. Totally symmetrical, with façades like those of an ancient temple, it is dominated at the center by a dome (altered during construction) and opens onto the countryside on all four sides.

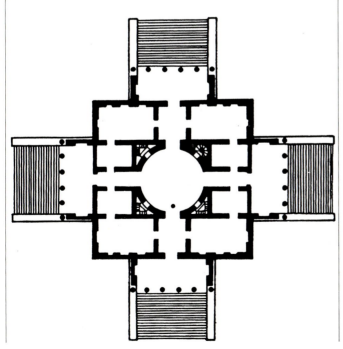

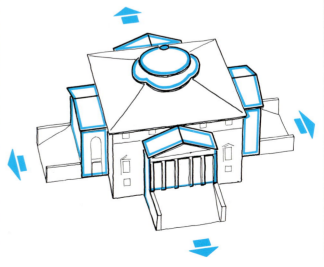

orders – a far more logical and coherent model.

Toward the end of the 15th century, a third and more refined type of palace appeared, with windows superimposed above each other. The prototype for this was Palazzo Farnese, built by Antonio da Sangallo and Michelangelo. This is a much less "rhythmical" building than Alberti's, its floors being indicated only by a decorated band, a stringcourse, and the façade completed with a large cornice. The orders are still present and used one above the other but they are seen only at the windows,

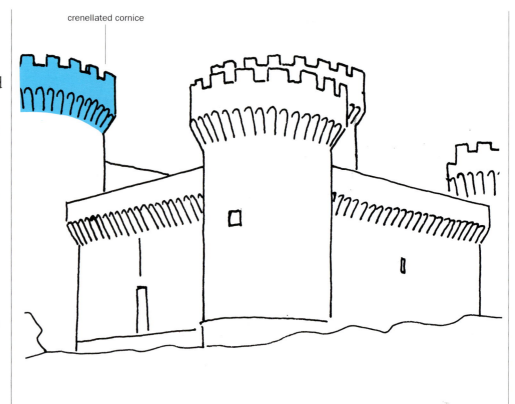

crenellated cornice

each one a miniature building in itself, complete with cornice and pediment (the triangular section beneath the roof). In other words, the architecture of the entire façade is condensed into a single element, the window, which absorbed all the functions. Of the three solutions this is clearly the most refined and remained a model for centuries. In church architecture there was scope for innovation in the design of both the façade and the plan, although in very different terms from those of the palace. It was not hard to come to

An invention: the stronghold

Villas were being built as residences so the stronghold was designed for defense. The towers were round, sturdy, and generally lower to withstand cannonballs; a projection running around the whole building enabled defenders to drive back attackers.

Above
The rocca of Tivoli.

Left
Filarete, the hospital (now part of the State University) of Milan: the courtyard.

Opposite page
The ducal courtyard in the Castello Sforzesco, Milan.

WOODEN INLAY

Already applied in the Middle Ages, the art of *intarsia*, inlay decoration with different colored woods, acquired great importance in the Renaissance, passing from simple ornamental motifs to more complex decorations, more typical of the art of painting, and the reproduction of illusionistic effects. The application of the principles of linear perspective was decisive in the evolution of this art, as they responded admirably to the demands of this technique, one that necessarily involved a geometrical simplification of form and the reduction of figure modeling to a few planes – the number permitted by the number of woods available (greatly limited compared with painting and so sometimes painted wood was used). Thanks to all these characteristics, inlay became an excellent medium for perspective art and was practiced mainly by architects and exploited for virtuoso decorations. Alessandro Baldovinetti was probably responsible for the design of the inlay on the cupboards in the sacristy of Florence cathedral.

a standard definition – or number of standard definitions – for the façade. The matter was addressed and the general factors resolved by Alberti. The façade of Santa Maria Novella had already been partly built when he designed its completion, giving it a Renaissance imprint. The fact that his design was superimposed on the existing façade without obliterating it determined its essential features. These include a framework of architectural orders uniting the upper and

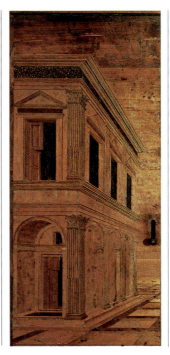

Left
Wooden inlay in Palazzo Ducale, Urbino.

Below
Giuliano da Sangallo, Villa Poggio a Caiano, Florence. Built for Lorenzo de'Medici, this house stands on a porticoed basement, similar to those of the villas of Pompei; an upper balustrade runs around the building and is reached up a horse shoe staircase. The façade has a number of windows and opens at the front in an Ionic portico; the pediment bears the Medici coat-of-arms.

lower parts of the façade and, in particular, two large S-shaped volutes that connect the wide bottom with the top, which is narrower because it corresponds to the width of the central nave. This simple and functional element was also to reach the height of its success in later centuries, especially in the Baroque period. A more refined, and more characteristic, example of Alberti's architecture is the façade of Sant'Andrea in Mantua. The forerunner of this type of façade was the

Urban studies

Renaissance artists took a great interest in ideal town planning although little was achieved because of technical difficulties.

Perhaps the most significant example is the Piazza Ducale in Vigevano. The whole is based on the consistent repetition of a single model: a wide arch at

street level, an arched window on the first floor and a small round window on the second floor.

The design of the Piazza Ducale in Vigevano is traditionally attributed to the great Leonardo da Vinci. Although it leads to the entrance of the large castle behind, the piazza was an accomplishment in its own right, considered the heart of the ideal town by Renaissance architects.

Roman triumphal arch, which met a similar functional requirement, that of a structure with a passage through its center. It is, however, clear that the architect found a far more sophisticated and complex solution to the organization of the façade with orders. He used them not one above the other but interposed. In the middle of the façade a pair of pilasters topped with an arch reveals the structure of the interior (articulated in just this way). This combination of arch and pilasters is itself part of a larger scheme, a "giant" order, in which the height of the main pilasters are determined by the total height of the smaller unit. Alberti had probably intended to repeat this motif above, on a smaller scale, but only the central arch was completed. The problem of the façade could therefore be resolved quite easily, as in these models. More complicated was the problem presented by the general structure of the building. Traditionally, Christian churches had been built on a Latin cross plan, which was appropriate both structurally and for liturgical purposes. However, it was not very compatible with the general trends of the Renaissance because there was – nor could

there be – no general rule as to the proportions of the arms of the cross. The tradition of the cross-shaped church was so deeply ingrained however that it proved impossible suddenly to abandon it. Initially, and for almost the whole of the 15th century, architects merely altered the interior, varying the distribution of spaces. Once the great cross vaults of Romanesque and Gothic churches were eliminated, the roof of the nave became

flat. Massive walls and large piers were no longer needed and, as in the first centuries of Christianity, church walls were built simple and straight, sustained by columns connected by round arches. These walls could be plastered, leaving the stone visible only at the entablatures, and these long straight bands of stone altered the impression given by the interior of the church. Instead of a succession of identical but clearly separate elements, there was now

a series of lines converging on a single point. Here, the second fundamental development of Renaissance art, perhaps even more important than the return to the theory of the orders and ancient forms, appeared: perspective. Much discussed in the 15th century, it was again Filippo Brunelleschi who produced a practical demonstration and the rules for its application. This technique made it possible, with the aid of

Donato Bramante, tempietto of San Pietro in Montorio, Rome.

174

scientific rules, to fix three-dimensional reality on the two dimensions of a flat surface. This enabled the architect to design a work of art and show a drawing of how it would look. Moreover, because perspective depended on a fixed viewpoint, the geometric center, the most important point in a building, tended increasingly to be also the center of the perspective. Between the late 15th and early 16th centuries Renaissance architects managed to create perfectly symmetrical and regular buildings in which all the principal lines converged on one central point. This was also the point from which the whole building could be seen at the same time, either because actually visible or because the part out of sight, being exactly the same as the part visible, could be imagined. The most refined type of Renaissance church, had a Greek cross (with four

Biagio Rossetti, the so-called Palazzo dei Diamanti in Ferrara. All the external façades of this building, constructed in 1492 for Duke Sigismondo d'Este, are decorated with blocks of diamond-pointed stone, hence the name given to the building. This is a typical example of an architectural approach greatly concerned with decoration, quite common in Emilia-Romagna, where northern influence starts to appear.

Decorative trends

Although the Renaissance style is one of the most rational, there are examples of delightful decorative accomplishments, characteristically obtained not with the uncontrolled distribution of ornament but the application of a single motif. The illustration on the left shows a decoration produced by the multiplication of thick rustication, a facing in shaped stone, on all the available façade space.

The exuberance of north Italy

The Renaissance arrived later in northern Italy than in the rest of the country. Moreover, it adopted a different form, in some ways the forerunner of what was seen in the next century in the rest of Europe, when Renaissance culture was transplanted to an environment with very different traditions.

All the architecture produced in northern Italy by Renaissance artists reveals the total supremacy of omnipresent decoration and exuberance over pure architecture. Indeed the whole architectural framework was covered by an abundance of sculptures, marble inlays, friezes and decorations.

equal arms) or circular plan. In either case, there was a central dome emphasizing the fact that this was the point of greatest importance. This arrangement was not very convenient in liturgical terms, because a large number of people had their backs to the altar, but it was adopted for aesthetic reasons, and churches of this type are exquisite creations. The palace and the church were the two principal Renaissance construction types but not the only ones; at least two others developed in these years. Curiously, these originated from the division of a single type. In the Middle Ages the castles of the nobility

had been scattered over the countryside and served both military and domestic purposes. By the 15th century the countryside, at least in Italy, had become relatively safe. Noblemen and rich citizens started to build not castles but villas, comfortable houses overlooking the countryside in which to rest away from their affairs. There was of course still a need for military garrisons, but these were housed in purpose-built constructions. This led to the birth of the *rocca*, or military stronghold, and soon it was designed with due consideration for the destructive power of firearms, increasingly common and more fearful. The best Italian architects now applied themselves to the design of the villa and the stronghold. The principles they developed were adopted in the construction of fortifications for

centuries – right up to the present – and splendid villas quickly appeared throughout the Italian peninsula. Around Venice, in particular, the villa became the principal building type and the field of activity of one of the greatest architects in the history of the art, Andrea Palladio. Two other trends complete this brief outline of Renaissance architecture. The first was the desire to rationalize town planning in the same way as had been done for single buildings, although more was achieved than building the architectural heart of the city, the piazza. But this was already a fine achievement and the efforts made formed the basis of modern urban planning, partly because, characteristically, the Renaissance did not adopt the albeit perfected ancient systems, preferring instead to develop new

ones. The second trend concerns style. Renaissance architecture originated in central Italy while Gothic was still being used in the north. When Renaissance influence did spread north of the Apennines the architects developed a less rigorous and more decorative style but this influence was really only seen in other countries. When the French invaded Italy at the end of the 15th century, the first Renaissance architecture they encountered was that of the north, close to their own taste and the first

they copied. For a certain period this "minor" school was better known and appreciated than the original. This anticipated the evolution of all Renaissance art, which moved away from constant experimentation toward an almost mechanical application of the splendid results attained, a development known as Mannerism. This, however, was a later occurrence. At that time Europe, after two thousand years, had something that could stand proudly beside the Parthenon.

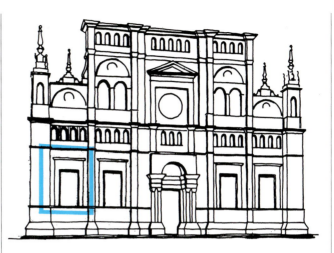

G. A. Amadeo, façade of the Certosa of Pavia. Highly decorated and applied to the façade of a Gothic church, this is one of the most characteristic examples of the application of forms elaborated in Tuscany in the north. This type of monument was the first to be seen by the French during the Italian wars and therefore made the greatest impression.

SCULPTURE

Unlike the Greeks, Renaissance artists never felt a need to draw up a set of rules for sculpture comparable to those followed in architecture. This is not to say that Renaissance sculpture lacks its own forms and trends, but simply that the transition from the art of the preceding century was less abrupt, and more a matter of taste than theory. The sculpture of the Renaissance was distinguished more by the ideas that inspired it. These were strong naturalism, expressed in a constant search for realism; great interest in the form of the human body and its potential for expression; a marked taste not only for greater knowledge and improved techniques but also the display of this knowledge; a yearning for monumentality; and a preference for geometrically simple compositions.

One idea that for centuries had been the most striking feature of European sculpture was now abandoned – its integration with the other arts, architecture in particular. The fact is that this was no longer possible. For a long time architecture had served as a setting for the other arts. During the Renaissance it lost that function as a building came to be thought of as a theorem, a product of the intellect to which ornamentation would add nothing; on the contrary, it would disturb. The architect no longer turned to the sculptor, painter, or glassmaker to enrich his buildings; instead he did all he could to reduce or eliminate their contribution, which was considered unnecessary or even detrimental to the appreciation of his model of mathematics and logic. Although never actually taken to the extreme, statues and paintings were confined to certain set places and enclosed in niches, clearly perceived as additions. In this way the architects of the time deprived sculpture of the position it had formerly occupied and greatly limited its scope as a form of architectural decoration. The sculptors partly approved and partly endured this approach but they soon reacted, changing the content

Interest in nature

Lorenzo Ghiberti, Gates of Paradise, Baptistery, Florence. Splendid frames with festoons of flowers, fruit and animals were used by Ghiberti to decorate the door (praised by his contemporaries as worthy of Paradise) and reveal the new style's respect for the world of nature. Also typical is the division into large square panels rather than small quatrefoiled ones.

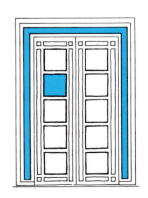

and application of their works and above all fixing more ambitious goals than mere integration in an architectural setting. The first and most essential of these was naturalism, the attempt to achieve the truest rendering of physical reality, which is seen in the work of all Renaissance sculptors. This was only to be expected, for whereas previous art forms had been steeped in mysticism the rational culture of the period was more concerned with depicting reality. Moreover, statues no longer had to fit into an architectural framework and were regarded as beautiful objects in their own right; it was only natural that sculptors should wish to abandon rigid models and favor greater spontaneity. This emphasis on naturalism also brought increased interest in man because to the Renaissance mind, as to that of classical antiquity, man was "the measure of all things," the noblest and most important creature in the universe. The human body, it is true, had been one of the main themes of medieval art, but more in a symbolic, distorted sense, as a "character." The sculptors of the Renaissance saw man as a creature made of muscles and bone. Donatello, the greatest sculptor of the 15th

Andrea del Verrocchio, David; Florence, Museo Nazionale del Bargello.

Interest in man
The utmost importance attributed by the humanists to man was translated into images that represent him as "truly" as possible. This principle seems to be the continuation of the interest in nature. The curved, sinuous lines that prevail in reality started to appear in art too.

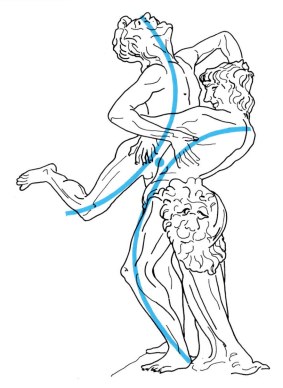

century, was probably the first artist since the Roman Empire to dare portray a naked human body. The sculpture had probably been modeled from life, using one of the Florentine boys who bathed naked in the Arno. This was a revolutionary creation, all the more so for the gently shaped curve – or *contrapposto* – of its outline, reminiscent of Greek sculpture. *Contrapposto* models were, at least in this sense, unknown to Gothic art but became the rule of that of the Renaissance. Naturalism, realism, observation of the human figure, the study of anatomy and compositional models based on the combination and contrast of curves – these are the main but

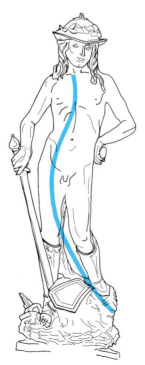

Above
Andrea del Verrocchio, Putto with Dolphin; *Florence, Palazzo Vecchio.*

Left
Donatello, David.

Opposite page
Antonio del Pollaiuolo, Hercules and Antaeus; *both bronzes are in the Bargello in Florence. After the fall off the Roman Empire David was probably the first nude statue in the round produced by European art. The naturalness of the whole and the realistic movements of Hercules and Antaeus reveal the characteristic Renaissance interest in man as he appears in real life.*

not the only features of Renaissance sculpture. Added to these was the continual study of technique in the attempt both to improve existing methods and to experiment with new ones. Renaissance sculptors achieved brilliant results in both respects and were able to create precisely the desired form in whatever material they chose, whether marble, stone, bronze, wood, or terra-cotta, without allowing technical difficulties to stop them. At the same time they invented new methods for the design and execution of their works. The most significant of these was perspective, which was applied not only to architecture but also to all art forms, including sculpture and painting. It revolutionized drawing, the common basis for all the arts. In sculpture it enabled the artist to perfect the study of realism and render perfectly natural proportions and poses; above all, figures could be grouped together while maintaining a realistic spatial relationship between them. It was therefore essential in the design of group sculptures and reliefs, in which the composition and background, the impression of real space around the figures, was paramount. Donatello introduced a further innovation, a technique known as *stiacciato* or *schiacciato*, which became commonly used in Renaissance low relief. Usually the sculptor varied the degrees of projection of the relief to give an impression of foreground, middle distance, and background. This technique involved differences that were a matter of millimeters but successfully created a sense of depth. If you imagine

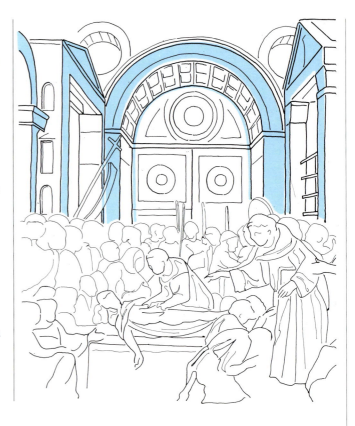

Display of technical skill
Donatello, Miracle of the Miser's Heart*; Padua, church of Sant'Ambrogio. Totally new techniques such as perspective and updated traditional ones such as stiacciato (compression of the different planes in low-relief) appeared in the work of sculptors. This famous example clearly reveals the use of perspective to lend depth.*

Left
Donatello, The Penitent Magdalene, *detail; Florence, Museo dell'Opera del Duomo.*

THE BAPTISMAL FONT IN THE CATHEDRAL OF SIENA AND JACOPO DELLA QUERCIA

The ideal way to assess the originality of Jacopo della Quercia is to observe the baptismal font in the cathedral of Siena, on which he worked alongside Donatello and Ghiberti. This work, commissioned in 1416 but not completed until 1434, is a marble tabernacle surrounded by niches containing the prophets and topped with a statue of John the Baptist. Below is a hexagonal basin, the sides of which are decorated with gilded bronze reliefs interspersed with niches containing figures of the Virtues by different artists. Jacopo was the last to deliver his panel (*Annunciation to Zacharias*, in the photograph) and after having seen the previous ones. However he adopted nothing from that of Ghiberti (*Arrest of the Baptist; Baptism of Christ*) and only external details from Donatello's (*Feast of Herod*). His predecessors concern with the scientific rendering of spatial perspective were alien to him: the altar steps are on the flat and the figures push the architecture back without occupying it. He was far more interested in the vitality of the human figure, enhanced by their monumentality, and filled with energy, the robes surging in independent motion. If one common denominator can be found in Jacopo's restless and still problematic work, this is a bursting vitality in his characters that engulfs and reconciles all the cultural references, whether Gothic, Burgundian, or Classical.

the different levels of projection as the bellows of an old-fashioned camera, Donatello practically squeezed this so that the levels were brought closer together. These studies and achievements – in naturalism, realism, technical and design skills – led in the 15th century to the reappearance of a sculptural form that had flourished in classical times but had subsequently virtually disappeared: the equestrian statue. Although some never

got beyond the design stage, two that were completed were of outstanding importance, masterpieces that opened the way to countless others and a genre that is still flourishing. They are also perhaps the most important works of their times and embody all the elements typical of the Renaissance: naturalism and realism in the minutely accurate study and rendering of the horse, its harness, and the details of the

Nanni di Banco, St. Luke; Florence, Museo dell'Opera del Duomo.

Donatello, St. John; Florence, Museo dell'Opera del Duomo.

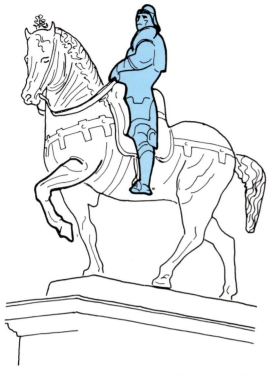

Below
Donatello, equestrian
monument of Gattamelata;
Padua, Piazza del Santo.
In monuments such as this,
the powerful and precisely
realistic portrayal of horse
and rider are combined with
a certain amount of
abstraction, for instance in
the presentation of the
condottiere – a soldier of
fortune - in the dress of an
ancient Roman.

Above
Monumentality
Andrea Verrocchio,
equestrian monument of
Bartolomeo Colleoni;
Venice, Campo di Santi
Giovanni e Paolo. The
Renaissance had two
distinctive characteristics:
realist portrayal and
monumental and complex
content. Here, actual
proportions of horse and
rider are preserved, and the
face of the soldier is a true
portrait.

horseman's armor. The interest in the man's body and his character is expressed in the splendid portraits of the face. The works also show an attraction to the monumental and the majestic. Another successful new device was the use of drawings in planning sculpture. There was an error in the design of the first statue as horse and rider were sculpted according to their true proportions with the result that, seen from below, the horse appears more imposing than its rider. No such mistake was made in the second example, which took account of the point of observation. A final contributory factor was the individualistic and dynamic nature of Renaissance society. In what other period would they have dared to raise such monuments to individuals who were neither kings, nor saints, nor heroes, but *condottieri*, soldiers of fortune, and mercenaries? This was the 15th century. The following century, despite its vast array of painters and architects, produced few renowned sculptors, partly because they had to be giants to compare with the Renaissance "greats." The 16th century did, however, produce the greatest of them all, Michelangelo. He embodied and fulfilled the entire experience of Renaissance sculpture. Marked by a powerful, even exuberant and

Above left
Michelangelo, Pitti Madonna; *Florence, Museo Nazionale del Bargello.*

Above right
Michelangelo, detail of the Madonna of the Stairs; Florence, Casa Buonarroti.

Geometrical figures
Michelangelo Buonarroti, Pietà; Rome, St. Peter's. The pyramid composition was a favorite arrangement of the Renaissance. Here, Michelangelo sculpted Christ to smaller proportions than the Virgin Mary to convey the relationship of mother and son and, at the same time, to maintain the geometry of the group based on the pyramid.

exaggerated anatomy, an unequaled monumentality and prodigious technical skill that at times reached virtuosity as well as a sheer and declared love for the human body, his works are among the most famous in the history of art. They can be used to trace the whole evolution of sculpture in the second half of the Renaissance. His first achievements, at the turn of the century, were still essentially 15th-century works: serene, not intimidating despite their majesty and the draperies are full and soft. The use of chiaroscuro is not exaggerated and the anatomy is robust. Above all there is an almost total "smoothness," an indication of the care and patience applied to the finish of the marble (Michelangelo's favorite material). The figures are grouped in simple, geometrical arrangements; the *Pietà*, for instance (the only work signed by Michelangelo, who is said to have carved his name in a moment of anger after overhearing visitors attributing the work to another artist), is clearly arranged within the framework of a pyramid. As the years passed, however, his art underwent a number of changes. In later works, the muscles appear to swell, the bodies become contorted, the chisel marks are left visible, group compositions become increasingly complex, and sometimes the artist seems to have begun a statue one way, then changed his mind and produced a different composition from the same block. These are the signs of an art that has reached its limit. The study and rendering of human character through the expression and movements of the body had been the central theme of Renaissance sculpture and resulted in great new achievements. Now, under the impulse of a genius, it became apparent that no sculpture, however superbly executed, no movement of the human body, however exquisitely rendered, could convey the full measure of the human drama. But only by its greatness did the Renaissance realize its limits.

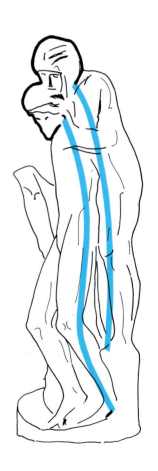

Free figures

A precise, rational scheme is never absent from Renaissance works, but it is not always geometric and imposed from the outside. Often it is soft and sinuous, adhering to the movement of the bodies portrayed. The movements of the figures may be lively but are never contorted or broken as in other periods of art history.

Left
Michelangelo, Moses, *detail; Rome, church of San Pietro in Vincoli, tomb of Pope Julius II.*

*Michelangelo Buonarroti,
Pietà; Milan, Castello
Sforzesco.
Begun in 1555, during the
last decade of the great
master's life, this is the last
Pietà by Michelangelo and
the most tormented. The
sculptor started one version
and then on the same block
of stone commenced
another. The rough finish of
the block is a characteristic
often found in late works by
this artist.*

PAINTING

Probably no other period in the history of art can boast the same wealth of achievement as the Renaissance.

The list of great painters includes Piero della Francesca, Fra Angelico, Masaccio, Botticelli, Mantegna, Leonardo, Michelangelo, Raphael, the Bellini brothers, Giorgione, Titian, Perugino, Paolo Uccello, Luca Signorelli, the two Lippis, the Ghirlandaio brothers, Cosmè Tura, Antonello da Messina and Carpaccio. They all came from the same country and the same era, yet each is worthy of the highest acclaim.

It would, nonetheless, be pointless to speak of Renaissance painting in European terms without due mention of the great masters from beyond the Alps: from the Germans Dürer and Cranach, who participated directly in Renaissance art and its trends, to the Flemish artist Van Eyck, whose research may have diverged from that of the Italians but was

Volume

Typical of much Renaissance painting is the continuing search for volume, a convincing three-dimensional effect in the figure. This concern was accompanied by a desire to place the figures in well-defined and appropriate surroundings. The use of perspective made a decisive contribution to the results.

equally important for the evolution of art in Italy as well. However brief, compared with other artistic movements, the Renaissance lasted for approximately two centuries and the works were varied and numerous. There was also great freedom and this was the first and most characteristic element of Renaissance painting – freedom from the rigid pre-established models of Gothic art and from the former constraints of frames

Masaccio, Tribute Money, details; Florence, church of the Carmine. Masaccio already presents most of the traits found in painting at the height of the Renaissance: monumentality, a faithful portrayal of the human body and proportion. The three-dimensional effect achieved *here is striking, as the painted figures look as if they are sculpted on the surface.*

Left
Detail of the figure of St. Peter.

or architectural settings. Although these conventions were not abandoned figures were "arranged" (not fitted within a frame) and the composition freer. The discovery of perspective had overwhelming effects although its adoption was gradual and, indeed, it was not always and integrally applied.
Only when incorporated in a totally realistic picture did it become essential. Painting is – or was thought to be – based on drawing so the discovery and application of

Opposite page
Andrea Mantegna, Arrival of Cardinal Francesco Gonzaga *(after restoration); Mantua, Palazzo Ducale, Camera Picta.*

Below
Vittore Carpaccio, Portrait of a Knight*; Madrid, Thyssen-Bornemisza collection.*

OIL PAINTING

Oil painting, previously thought to have been invented by Jan van Eyck, was probably already known in antiquity. It is mentioned in the writings of Theophilus (first half of the 12th century) and Cennini (late 14th century) although only from the middle of the 15th century did it really begin to spread. Although the most common form of support is canvas, the first oil paintings were on wood; the base was primed with gesso and glue, spread in fine crisscross layers and carefully sealed. The colors applied to this white base were obtained from earth, vegetable, or animal extracts or from minerals ground to a powder. The binding medium, however, and this was the innovation, was a common (walnut, linseed, poppyseed) or essential (turpentine, rosmary) oil. The latter produced a more fluid and transparent result, suited to glazing. The colors thus prepared dried slowly, making it easier to work and obtain softer shades, thus greatly increasing the color range to create stronger light contrasts and more striking effects. The paint could be applied in several manners – in a perfectly smooth polished finish or a rippled and tormented one, marked by the brush or spatula to lend expression in a textured surface (photograph: Jan van Eyck, *Rolin Madonna*, Paris, Musée du Louvre).

193

perspective made drawing the common basis for all the visual arts, permitting, indeed causing, the birth of the "design" which came to be considered the true essence of a work of art, more so than its execution. Drawing was used to test all the various artistic theories; its transformation into a painting was a short step.

In brief, from the Renaissance onward painting became the test bench for all artistic transformations. Second, during

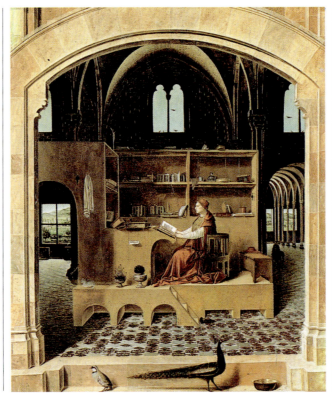

Above
Piero della Francesca, Flagellation of Christ; *Urbino, Palazzo Ducale. The arrangement of the figures is rigorously logical. But the reality is still that of theater; the figures are seen from the front, almost as if posing against the architecture. This mathematically constructed reality is typical of Renaissance art.*

Left
Antonello da Messina, St. Jerome in His Study, *detail; London, National Gallery.*

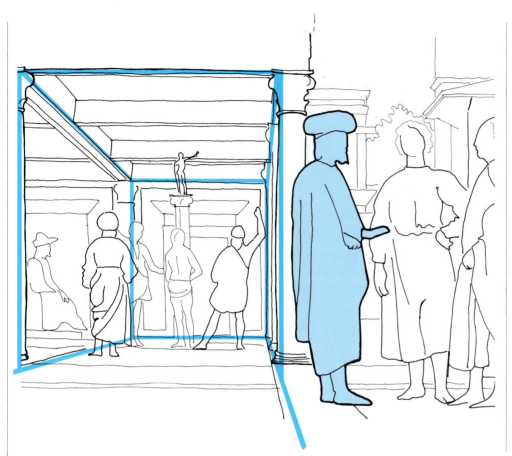

Volume: Piero della Francesca.

The distinctive features of Renaissance art are clearly visible in the work of Piero della Francesca, perspective being the fundamental component. The entire construction is almost mathematical; architecture is seen from the front, the blocks of figures are arranged in rectangles proportionate to those of the architecture and the two groups match.

Below
Piero della Francesca, Resurrection; Borgo San Sepolcro, Pinacoteca Comunale.

the 15th and 16th centuries various new techniques and materials were discovered that greatly increased the potential for expression, at the same time reducing the costs and efforts required to produce a painting or fresco. Toward the end of the 15th century, oils were introduced into Italy from the Low Countries. As well as proving easier to prepare and more precise than tempera, these facilitated the representation of reality, and Renaissance painters literally fell in love with them. At about the same time, canvas replaced wooden panels as the support for paintings, making the finished works more durable and easier to transport. The exploration of perspective through preparatory sketches was further encouraged by the introduction of two new graphic mediums – red chalk and pastel – which proved useful supplements to the pens, brushes, silver point and charcoal already available. The use of cartoons, or large

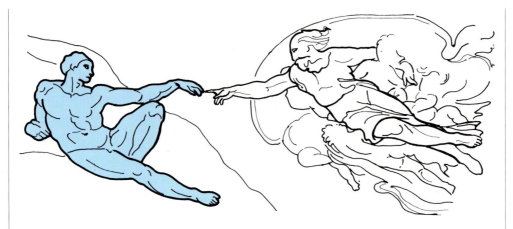

Volume: Michelangelo

The Renaissance concern with the study, appreciation, and expressive rendering of the human body was brought to a climax by Michelangelo. As often occurs at the end of a process, he even indulged in a slight exaggeration but the mastery of technique is splendid, with fine compositional arrangements – large curved lines instead of the previous geometrical blocks – and portrayal of the anatomy.

Below
Palma the Elder, Venus and Cupid; *Cambridge, Fitzwilliam Museum.*

Opposite page, bottom
Titian, Bacchus and Ariadne; *London, National Gallery.*

sheets of paper, made fresco painting much easier. Now the subject could be painted at leisure in the studio before being transferred to the plaster wall by means of dusting the back of the cartoon with charcoal and pressing the design through. Previously, the study had to be worked directly on to the plaster in broad outline and the final painting completed quickly.

What were the aims of this style and how were they expressed? It is difficult and perhaps misleading to reduce a movement that contained such a wealth of personalities, works, and trends to some form of model. Clearly, however, a common basis and themes did exist. All Western painting focuses on the portrayal of man and his environment and this applies to the Renaissance too. Its greatest innovation was the study of greater realism in the rendering of the subject. This was only logical, as the whole culture of the times was occupied with an interest in man, nature and their appearance. Renaissance painters can be divided into two main groups as far as the portrayal of man and his surroundings are concerned.

The results achieved by each of these are absolutely and characteristically Renaissance but the forms are quite different.

The artists of the first group or school can somewhat arbitrarily be labeled, for the sake of convenience, as "innovators." This definition is justified by the fact that as well as having made

the biggest break with earlier art, their work expressed most completely the values of the new era. They also provided a source of inspiration for the artists that followed them. What interested them above all was the human figure in its physical reality. If one characteristic of their work were to be singled out, it would be "volume". Previously, through lack of knowledge or technical ability, figures had been depicted in silhouette, lacking depth and almost as if cut out and placed on a quite unrealistic, usually gilded background.

This now changed; the new technique of perspective meant that surroundings could be portrayed more realistically and with extreme precision. The spirit of the times led artists to adopt a more profound interest in man, placing him in a well-defined, identifiable setting. There are many ways to do this but characteristically the new art used drawing; the figures and scenery are colored drawings. This school started with the work of the great 15th-century artist Masaccio, who, although he was to die before the age of

Michelangelo Buonarroti, The Creation of Adam, detail, ceiling of the Sistine Chapel; Rome, Vatican. Landscape is reduced to a minimum with all the attention centered on the figures of Adam and the Creator. The artist had no models for these but his knowledge of anatomy was such that he created the images, accentuating certain parts to make the subject even more "natural."

197

thirty, was considered by contemporaries as the Brunelleschi of painting, the creator of a new style. The most obvious and significant characteristics of his small but exceptional output are the solidity, serene majesty, and sheer monumentality of his figures.
Movements are few and measured and some figures are completely immobile and upright, but each occupies his own clearly perceived space, a three-dimensional presence against the background of the painting, the "scenario" (in much 15th-century painting subjects were treated like actors on an imaginary stage).
In the early Renaissance the many artists of this school included Piero della Francesca.

Left
Fra Angelico, Triptych of St Peter Martyr, *detail; Florence, Museo di San Marco.*

Opposite page, top
Fra Angelico. Annunciation, illumination; Florence, Museo di San Marco.

Above
Masolino da Panicale, Healing of the Lame Man, *detail (after restoration); Florence, church of Santa Maria del Carmine, Brancacci Chapel. Masolino and Masaccio were commissioned to decorate the chapel in 1424 by Felice Brancacci, a rich silk merchant actively involved in public life and the sea trade.*

His work featured monumental figures and reveals a concern with the "mathematical" construction of the landscape and surroundings, another characteristic of the Renaissance. The height of this trend was to come with Michelangelo. In his works the characteristically massive figures sometimes became "explosive," so powerful and heroic were his portrayals of the human body, and indeed this was practically his sole obsession.

Another contrasting group that also lasted

Below

Fra Angelico, Annunciation, *detail; Madrid, Prado.*

Grace

The second current of Renaissance painting comprised painters who applied the new techniques to update ancient models, using beauty of line and elegant images.

throughout the Renaissance period flanked this innovative school of painters. These artists were on the whole more conservative, and reluctant to abandon completely the splendid achievements of their predecessors and particularly loved the dreaminess, joy, beautiful colors and grace of Gothic painting. If their work had to be described in a single word, it would be elegance. They achieved this by a skilful mastery of "line," by designing shapes with graceful outlines. The artists

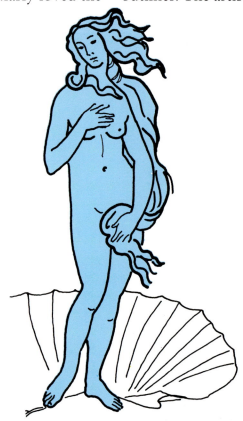

Sandro Botticelli, Birth of Venus, *detail; Florence, Uffizi.*
The elegance of figure, with flowing locks and graceful pose, in pictures such as this replaced the volume and plasticity found in the work of Masaccio or Piero della Francesca.

200

in this group, which included Fra Angelico, Botticelli and Cranach, by no means rejected the new discoveries and lessons of the Renaissance – perspective, naturalism and the study of anatomy. But their concern was principally applied to elegance of gesture, drapery, and color rather than to the depiction of a seemingly harsh physical reality. One group was attracted to graceful lines and fabulous or dreamlike backgrounds, and the other gave prominence to severity, vigor and monumentality. What differed was how the picture was perceived. For some it was a sort of stage and there were three main factors – the space defined by the scenography (architecture, mountains, nature), the position of the figures within this space and the importance of the individual figure in its group. For the others – those defined as "conservative" – the support was essentially a surface on which to portray scenes with the aid of drawing and color. Here, it was the painting that counted

Lucas Cranach the Elder, Adam; Florence, Uffizi. Foreign artists such as Cranach preferred a type of painting based more on linear values and color than on the rendering of space and depth. This is not surprising because, despite some obvious differences, this approach was closer to the art traditions north of the Alps. Cranach typically adopted a uniform background, blue, tobacco, or pale green, against which to set his figures.

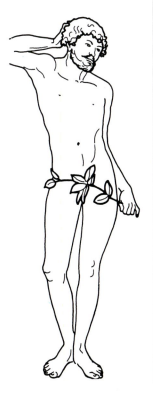

201

rather than the subject matter. This very brief summary of the different methods used to represent a story, an event, or a situation has not dealt with another genre, practically invented during the Renaissance and destined to become very successful. This was portrait painting.

Medieval artists had painted portraits but they had been asked only to portray the sitter's role, not his personality or features; in other words, the symbol rather than the man. The Renaissance

Above
Lorenzo Lotto, Messer Marsilio and His Bride, *detail; Madrid, Prado.*

The portrait

Antonello da Messina, Portrait of a Man, *presumed self-portrait; London, National Gallery.*
Along with its interest in the individual, the Renaissance developed that for portraiture, characteristically showing the head and shoulders. Initially the subject was drawn from the side, but this quickly changed to a three-quarters view (as here) with the figure set against a dark background.

could not share such an approach, quite the reverse of its philosophy, in which man, the individual, was the force behind history, culture and progress. When patrons began to demand pictures that were true likenesses, painters were prepared to supply them. At first, as occurs in all new experiences, the expressiveness of portraiture was limited by lack of technical knowledge. The sitter was shown only in profile and staring straight ahead. The artistic results were exceptional and the rendering of physical and psychological characteristics excellent usually, but ultimately the style is artificial, arbitrary and extremely limited.

No one is ever normally seen in this way. What is more, it showed that the artist had not yet overcome the habit of presenting a subject flat against a background. Only the background looked real, a landscape drawn accurately in line and color. At the same time, the face had undergone a similar process and was no longer a cardboard

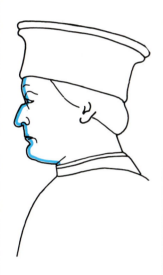

Piero della Francesca, Portrait of Federico da Montefeltro; *Florence, Uffizi. This is the earliest type of 15th-century portrait. The model is seen from the side, in profile; this may be a simple solution but it is not very realistic even though the features are faithfully reproduced. Moreover, the artist was still reluctant to focus entirely on the human figure, inserting it in a fascinating – but distracting – natural environment.*

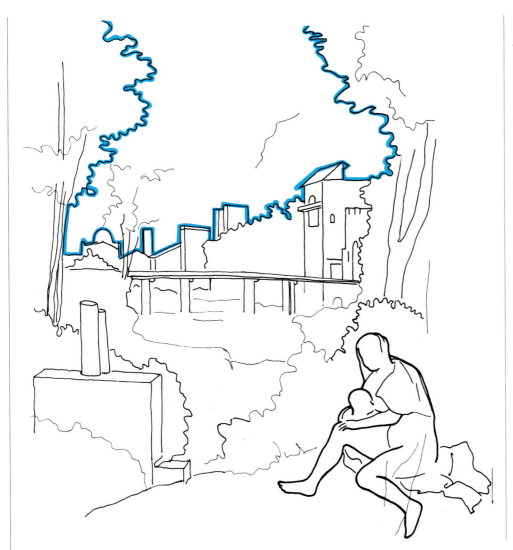

The introduction of nature
An interest in the aspects of the natural world led to the appearance of scenery and sometimes the reproduction of natural phenomena. Here it is a thunderstorm.

Below
Giovanni Bellini, Feast of the Gods; *Washington, National Gallery of Art. Born of the artist's fantasies in the later years of his life, this masterpiece was executed for Alfonso d'Este's "alabaster chamber"; the landscape was later altered by Titian although he did not change the atmosphere of a calm and archaic mythological fable.*

outline but realistic, a credible study of features. Within a few decades, painters had learned how to present their models in the far more natural three-quarters pose that is seen from the front but slightly side-on. Increasingly confident of their new·skills, they replaced landscapes with plain dark backgrounds that showed off their subjects more effectively. Oils, with their soft, warm colors, were gradually adopted in place of tempera, cold and smooth-surfaced, which had proved less than ideal for lifelike portraits. Although the evolution of landscape painting as a separate genre was not to be completed until after the Renaissance, it too became increasingly important in its own

right. In a certain sense it countered the development of the portrait and developed in two directions. On the one hand, there was an emphasis on the pleasures and delights of the countryside and, on the other, a concern with the features, real or imagined, of the townscape. The most famous examples of this are the paintings of Venice, depicting its inhabitants going about their daily lives or enjoying the city festivities. The imaginary aspect gradually grew in importance and gave rise to painted decoration using mock architecture showing the ceilings of churches and palaces. The 15th and 16th centuries

Giorgione, The Tempest, detail; Venice, Accademia. For the painters of central Italy the picture was a colored drawing whereas the Venetian artists perceived it principally as a combination of colors based on a drawing. For this reason they attributed less importance to line and rigorous perspective, basing their work on the skillful use of color. In this Giorgione achieved a major technical success – tonal painting, obtaining effects of light and shade and volume by varying the degrees of dull or bright colors.

produced fine examples of both these genres but it is important to note that none of the many fine landscapes and townscapes excludes the human figure completely or reduces it merely to the role of an accessory; this was a later development. Throughout the Renaissance the interest in man was extremely strong, he always appeared physically and as the, most obvious, subject of the painting. When interest was focused on the presentation of architecture, perspective sometimes became so important as to seem the main purpose, almost as if the painting had been created to show off the possibilities of this new technique. Usually, the lines are shown converging toward a single vanishing point, and often the artist seems to have invented a complex structure simply to demonstrate this achievement.
An example of this is the ceiling fresco creating the illusion of a circular skylight; the figures placed all

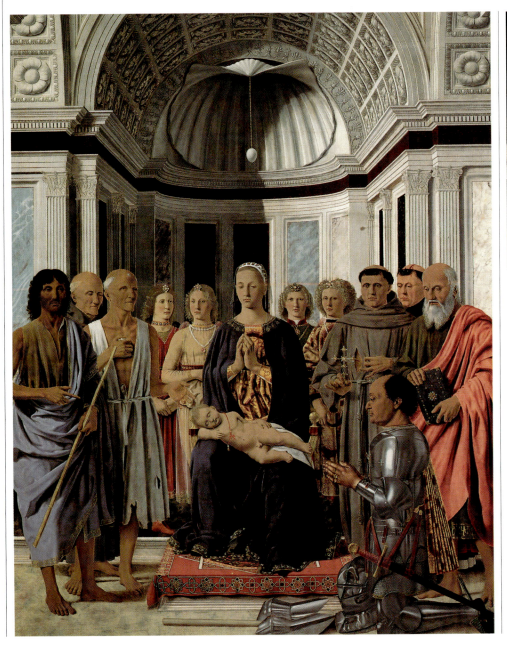

Piero della Francesca, Madonna and Child with Saints, *detail; Milan, Pinacoteca di Brera. Executed again for the Duke of Montefeltro, who appears in shining armor, despite its precise rendering of perspective this composition appears freer and to have more movement. This is partly because of the slightly different projection created between the perspective of the monumental architecture and that of the semicircle of saints around the throne.*

around guide the eye to the center. Most Renaissance paintings were religious in origin and subject. Representations of the saints, episodes from the Bible, and symbolic or ritual studies abounded. Commissions kept the art alive and there are numerous examples of Renaissance paintings on each of these subjects.

The subject commissioned most often was the Virgin and Child.

There was scarcely a 15th-or 16th-century painter who did not produce at least one or two versions, but for some – such as Raphael – it became their principal subject. Naturally, styles of expression were of endless variety and interpretations manifold.

But a single element dominated, inspired by tradition and at the same time in harmony with the new ideas of majesty and functionality, and dictated by the nature of the subject: the arrangement of the two figures – Mother and Child – in the shape of a pyramid. The Virgin's feet and the folds of her mantle formed the base of the structure; her head was at its top.

This was the set model characteristic of the Renaissance Madonna.

The many sophisticated variations on this approach included ones which chose to show certain parts of the body turned in different directions. In a seated figure, for example, the feet could be turned to the right and the head to the left, lending movement and life to the picture. Another approach – in which Leonard da Vinci proved a master – involved the use chiaroscuro, the

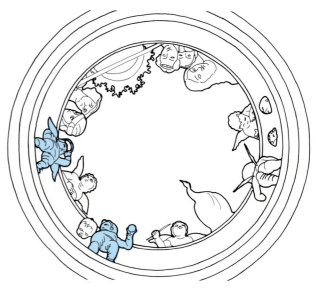

The display of perspective
Andrea Mantegna, ceiling fresco, Camera Picta; Mantua, Palazzo Ducale. Perspective was the main concern in this painting, the first of a large number using tricks of perspective to decorate the ceilings of palaces and churches. The fresco portrays a large opening in the ceiling, with various figures and animals looking down.

207

technique of conveying the shapes of figures not so much with lines as through contrasts of light and shade, and subtle gradations of light and dark.
The latter technique is called *sfumato*, and the effect is that of a picture seen through a veil.
In summary these are the models, the forms and methods adopted to create the most characteristic and easily recognized compositional elements of Renaissance painting. Art galleries throughout the world are filled with the incredible genius of Renaissance painting.
It did more than simply establish artistic rules and guidelines that are still applied today, it brought to an end the

Above
Leonardo da Vinci, Lady with an Ermine; *Cracow, Narodni Muzei.*
A lively portrait of Ludovico il Moro's favorite, Cecilia Gallerani; the figure, flooded with light, emerges from the shadowy background in a spiral effect that enhances both volume and grace.

Opposite page
Compositional figures
Raphael, Virgin with Goldfinch; *Florence, Uffizi.*
In paintings and statues alike, the pyramidal composition was by far the most commonly adopted, especially for the sacred groups much in vogue at the time. Often a landscape or architectural background is added or forms part of it.

THE WRITINGS OF LEONARDO

Leonardo's *Treatise on Painting*, a collection of notes, thoughts and reflections on the relationship between art and science put together by a follower, proves the total homogeneity of his scientific and painting interests – complementary and intimately interrelated parts of his work. The treatise clearly reveals the role of supreme "mental reasoning" assigned by Leonardo to painting and his high vision of the artist intended as the "master of all things that can happen in the thought of man." Some definitions and statements made by Leonardo on painting in this *Treatise* are quoted below:

"The painter cannot be praised if he is not universal."
"Oh wondrous science, you reserve in life transient beauty [...] continually changed by time."
"Observe the light and consider its beauty. Blink and look again: what you see before was not, and what was is no more."

Opposite page
Sfumato
Leonardo da Vinci, Madonna with a Carnation*; Munich, Alte Pinakothek. The great Leonardo mastered a highly unusual painting technique, that is* sfumato, *an effect so refined and gradual as to make the transition from light to shade gentle and imperceptible. This gives a highly distinctive character to his works, which seem almost viewed through a fine veil.*

Below
Leonardo da Vinci, Madonna and Child with St. Anne, *detail; Paris, Musée du Louvre.*

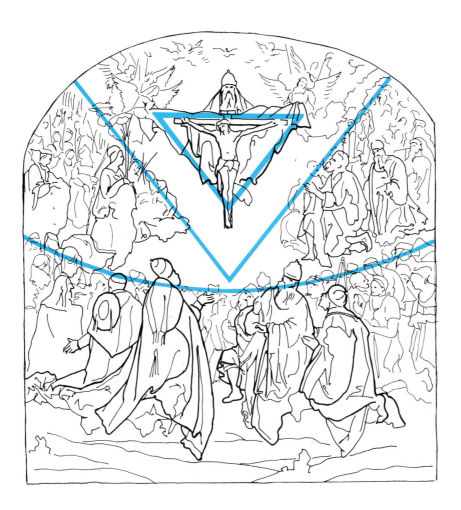

Geometrical figures in complex compositions
Albrecht Dürer, Adoration of the Trinity*; Vienna, Kunsthistoriches Museum.* One constant feature of the Renaissance period is the search for rational, logical and clear compositions. Renaissance works are always intelligently constructed according to strict geometric rules and much of their fascination undeniably lies in this.

Below
Albrecht Dürer, Feast of the Rosary*; Prague, Narodni Galerie.*

thousand-year history and culture of the Middle Ages. It was the beginning of the modern era. In just a few decades, one country produced more artists than others in their entire histories. No book can possibly convey the vitality and force of Renaissance art but this outline may serve as a first step towards an understanding and appreciation of one of history's most fertile, significant, interesting and vibrant periods.

Baroque Art

Baroque art was a product of the period spanning the 17th century and the early decades of the 18th century. Geographically, it covered most of Europe and Latin America, but its development and decline followed an irregular pattern from one country to another. Local characteristics were likewise very varied, despite a common origin; and so too was its popularity.

The reasons for these differences were both geographical and historical. Baroque developed at the beginning of the 17th century in papal Rome, where, rather than a clearly defined style, it was a tendency common to all the arts – a taste, a fashion. Later it spread to the rest of Europe and to Latin America, the typical Baroque forms appearing in these parts of the world after an interval that increased with their distance from Italy.

Where the cultural, religious, and political climate was similar to that of Italy, the Baroque style was

215

Francesco Castelli, known as Borromini, dome of San Carlo alle Quattro Fontane, Rome.
Grandiose constructions whith complex decoration; this could be the definition of Baroque architecture. Here the decoration of the dome is based on a complex combination of crosses, octagons and hexagons.

In the Cornaro chapel in Santa Maria della Vittoria in Rome, Bernini sought the integration of architecture, sculpture and painting in his portrayal of the ecstasy of St. Teresa, appealing to the spectator's senses and emotions.

216

popular and spread quickly; where it was not it was rejected. In both cases this wave of influence moved from Italy to encounter and fuse with local trends and schools. In this way many art forms of a national character were produced, each with its own peculiarities; these various art forms together constituted Baroque art. The results achieved in architecture, painting, and other disciplines were in no way inferior to their Italian counterparts. In some fields such as painting – suffice to name Rubens, Rembrandt, and Velázquez – they were far superior.

Thus Italy, while still at the forefront of artistic development in Europe at the beginning of the Baroque period, by the end it had lost its artistic supremacy, which had passed to France, where it was to remain.

As far as theory is concerned, the essential feature of Baroque art was a fundamental ambiguity. Baroque artists proclaimed themselves the heirs of the Renaissance and claimed to accept its rules, but they violated these systematically both in spirit and letter. The Renaissance meant equilibrium, moderation, sobriety, reason, logic: Baroque was movement, desire for novelty, love of the infinite and the non-finite, of contrasts and the bold fusion of all the arts. It was as dramatic, exuberant, and theatrical as the preceding period had been serene and restrained. In fact the two movements had quite different objectives and so the means used to attain them were also different, even directly opposed.

Renaissance art addressed reason and above all sought to convince: Baroque art, on the other hand, appealed to instinct, to the senses, the imagination, and sought to captivate. Not surprisingly it came into being as the artistic instrument of the Catholic Church, bent at that time on winning back heretics or at least on consolidating the faith of believers and impressing them with its own majesty.

ARCHITECTURE

Although examples of Baroque architecture are to be found virtually all over Europe and Latin America, they differ notably from one country to another. How is it, then, that they are all given the same name? Partly for convenience, in order to summarize the art of a whole period with a single word, but mainly on account of their common aesthetic origin.

In Spain the term *Baroque* originally denoted an irregular, bizarre-shaped pearl, whereas in Italy it meant a pedantic, contorted argument of little dialectic value. It ended by becoming, in almost all European languages, a synonym for the extravagant, deformed, abnormal, unusual,

absurd, and irregular, and in this sense it was adopted by 18th-century critics to apply to the art of the previous century, which seemed to them conspicuously to possess such characteristics.

In the second half of the 19th century the Swiss critic Heinrich Wölfflin and his followers gave the word a more objective meaning. Still referring to the art of the 17th and early 18th centuries, they defined as Baroque those works that contained certain specific characteristics: the use of movement, whether actual (a curving wall, a fountain with jets of water forever changing shape) or implied (a figure portrayed performing a vigorous action or effort), the attempt to

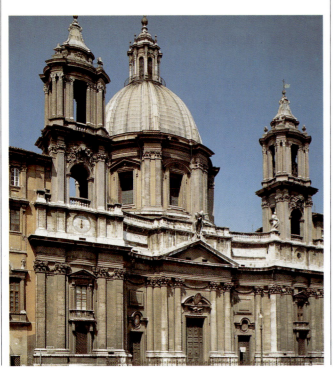

Left
Francesco Borromini, façade of the church of Sant'Agnese in Piazza Navona, Rome.
The architect transformed the existing Greek cross structure into an octagon, broken by chapels alternating with large buttresses. He set the dome on this, above a high drum; externally it is seen towering above the wide curve of the façade.

Scenographic effect
Of all the churches he designed, Sant'Andrea al Quirinale in Rome (right) was Gian Lorenzo Bernini's favorite and is typical of his style. It is marked by an acceptance of the Renaissance rules with the addition of one or two scenographic effects. In Baroque churches the center of the façade is more important than the sides. Here the façade wall is topped with an elegant circular half temple that ends in a high pediment and contains the curved lines typical of Baroque.

represent or suggest infinity (an avenue disappearing into the distance, a fresco giving the illusion of boundless sky, a trick of mirrors that altered perspectives and made them unrecognizable); the importance given to light and its effect in the conception of a work of art and the final impact created; the taste for theatrical, grandiose, scenographic effects; and the tendency to disregard the boundaries between the various forms of art and to mix together architecture, painting, and sculpture. Critically speaking, this is perhaps the best way to approach the problem because more than a style, Baroque is a taste, an attitude toward life and art; indeed we speak of Baroque music, Baroque theater and

even Baroque ceremonies and dress. The simplest way to approach the problem is to examine the buildings constructed in the 17th century and how their architects conceived them. In architectural terms, the attention of the age focused on two types of building: the church and the palace. The different versions included, respectively, cathedrals, parish churches, and monastic buildings and town or country mansions and, above all, royal palaces, the latter being typical of the period. In addition to these individual buildings, Baroque architecture was also characterized by what is now known as town planning: the arrangement of urban areas according to predetermined models

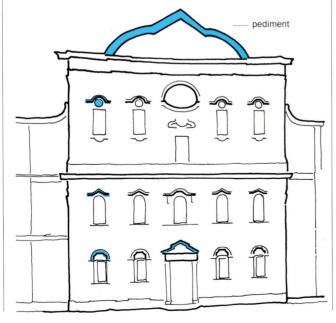

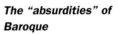
— pediment

The "absurdities" of Baroque

The Baroque style did not repudiate classical forms (columns, arches, pediments, friezes) but transformed them; no one did this more than Borromini. In this façade, for instance, the usual triangular or semicircular pediments – the upper part of the windows, doors and building itself – are broken, as in the central doorway, or have a mixture of straight, curved or angular lines connected together. Some even invert their function to appear "inside" instead of "above" the window aperture. Because of this approach, in the 18th century, Baroque artists were accused of seeking "license" and the "absurd."

Opposite page, top Filippo Regazzini, Piazza Sant'Ignazio in Rome.

and the creation of great parks and gardens around residences of importance. A building can be conceived in many different ways: as an ensemble of stories one above the other (the present attitude); as a box with walls of regular shape (as Renaissance architects understood it); or as a skeleton, one formed by the various structures needed to sustain it (the Gothic conception). Baroque architects saw it as a single mass to be shaped according to the

Francesco Castelli, known as Borromini, the Oratory of San Filippo Neri, Rome. As well as the apparent liberties taken with detail (actually only slightly different from those fixed by tradition), the curved façade of the oratory is typically Baroque. The lower part protrudes slightly, but above it traces a contrasting inward curve. The movement of the two parts is used to create a small balcony which, together with other details, helps to lend importance to the central part of the building. A similar effect sought at Sant'Andrea al Quirinale is obtained here with very different means.

requirements. In short, for Baroque architects a building was rather like a large sculpture. This conception had a cardinal effect on ground plans – the outline of a building as seen from above. It led to the rejection of the simple, elementary, analytical plans favored by Renaissance architects. Instead, the preference was for complex, rich, dynamic designs more appropriate to constructions that were no longer thought of as "built," or created by the union of various separate parts, but rather as "hollowed out," shaped from a compact mass in several stages. The plans common to Renaissance architecture were square, round and the Greek cross (a cross with four equal arms). Those typical of Baroque architecture were the ellipse, the oval or far more complex schemes based on complicated geometric figures. The Italian Francesco Castelli, better known by the name he adopted for himself Borromini, designed a church with a ground-plan in the shape of a bee, in honor of the patron who commissioned it, whose family coat of arms featured bees; and another with walls that were alternately convex and concave. One French architect went so

Pietro da Cortona, church of Santi Luca e Martina, Rome. Started in 1635, the reconstruction work on the church of the Accademia di San Luca was pursued by the artist after the discovery of the body of St. Martina and continued until 1650. The magnificent treatment of the surfaces, worked in relief with sunken columns and projecting pilasters, reflects the teachings of Michelangelo. It does not however exclude accentuated decoration or unusual combinations of curved and broken lines – particularly attractive in the fanciful creations on the interior and the exterior of the dome.

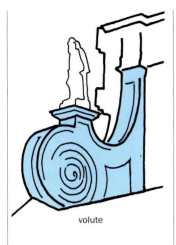

volute

Scroll buttresses

The church of Santa Maria della Salute in Venice is nothing special: a number of chapels brought together on an octagonal plan and crowned with a large hemispherical dome. One feature, however, distinguishes it: the large scrolls. These provide an organic solution to the connection of the large base to the narrow dome, giving the construction a unified outline, suited to its position.

Baldassare Longhena, Santa Maria della Salute, Venice. This imposing white church is more typical of Venice than of Baroque in general. However, the large scroll buttresses – known as orecchioni – that distinguish the exterior are also one of the most characteristic features of Baroque architecture. They are a brilliant solution to the problem of lending a classical appearance to the side buttresses needed for all domed roofs.

223

far as to propose ground plans for a series of churches forming the letters of the king's name, Louis Le Grand, as the Sun-King Louis XIV liked to be called. This search for complexity – or rather rejection of simplicity, unsuited to a conception of the building seen as a moulded block – led to the replacement of straight lines and flat surfaces (which tend inevitably to give the impression of a "box") with undulating lines and surfaces. As well as complex ground plans, the resultant curving walls were, therefore, the other outstanding characteristic of Baroque buildings. Not only did they respond to the vision of a building as a single entity, they also introduced another characteristic of the Baroque, the idea of movement, into architecture, which was by its very nature the most static of all the arts. And indeed, once discovered, the undulating motif was not confined to walls. The idea of giving movement to an architectural element in the form of more or less regular curves and counter curves became a dominant stylistic feature of all Baroque art. Interiors were made to curve – from the church of Sant'Andrea in the Quirinale by Gian Lorenzo Bernini, one of

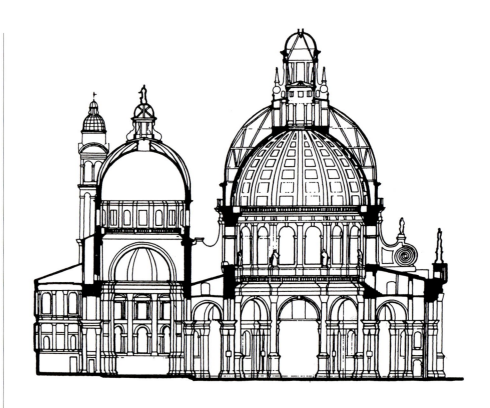

Above and bottom left
Baldassarre Longhena, section and plan of the church of Santa Maria della Salute, Venice. The plan of this church was created by juxtaposing elements on different levels: the octagon with the drum and dome; the presbytery, with two apses and topped with a second dome; the choir, separated from the presbytery by an arch on columns that defines the space of the main altar.

Below
Plan of the Karlskirche, Vienna.

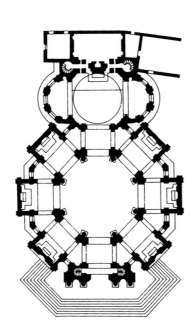

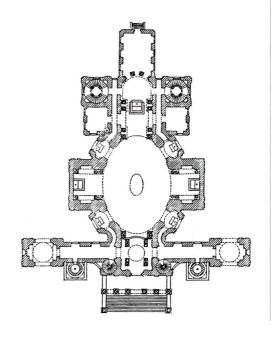

THE COLONNADE OF PALAZZO SPADA

The famous Colonnade (or perspective) of Palazzo Spada is perhaps the most curious example of the Baroque interest in the problems of space and perspective illusion. Described a "diabolical trick" by Erwin Panofsky, those viewing this small stucco-work gallery through the two doorways in the left wing of the palace from the courtyard have the impression that it is very deep but actually it is not even nine meters long. This effect is achieved by progressively reducing the internal space and the height of the two rows of columns that flank the corridor, creating a sort of inverted telescope. This work was commissioned by Cardinal Bernardino Spada who called upon two of the most admired artists of the times, Agostino Mitelli and Angelo Michele Colonna. He wanted to create an illusory extension of space and in order to do so, in 1653, turned to a scholar of perspective, Father Giovanni Maria Bitonto, and to Borromini. Today the Colonnade has been darkened by the closing of its windows but the effect must, in the past, have been very different and the short walk seemed a splendid passage between two gardens – one royal and still in existence, and another mock one beyond the gallery itself, with

a view of four flowerbeds and a number of trees frescoed on the back wall. Those who ventured in would discover the trick and have grasped the moral metaphor implicit in the play of perspective: to use the words of Cardinal Spada "the misleading image of the world" and its values "only apparently great," but which become "small at the moment you clasp hold of them." Aided by the science of Father Bitonto, Borromini adopted subtle tricks of perspective and to avoid an excessively accelerated sequence also created the illusion of side spaces that seem to interrupt the fluidity of the colonnade.

In 1646 Francesco Borromini was commissioned to renew the interior of the church of San Giovanni in Laterano on the condition that he maintain the ancient basilican structure and the 16th-century wooden ceiling. The architect demonstrated his great versatility in this design. He encased the columns of the arcade in piers alternating with broad arches and he unified the wall using a single row of huge pilasters from floor to ceiling.

The rhythm created by the alternating piers and arches was unbroken to the façade where slanting piers lead to the entrance, eliminating the right-angled separation.

the leading representatives and creators of Roman Baroque, to that of San Carlo alle Quattro Fontane or Sant'Ivo at the Sapienza by Borromini, his fierce rival. So too were facades, as in almost all Borromini's work; Bernini's proposal for the Palais du Louvre in Paris, and typically in the work of Italian, Austrian, and German architects. Even columns were designed to undulate. Those of Bernini's great baldacchino above the high altar of St. Peter's in Rome were only the first of a host of spiral columns to be placed in Baroque churches. The Italian architect Guarino Guarini actually evolved, and applied in some of his buildings (for example, and a church to be built in Lisbon), an "undulating order," in the form of a system of bases, columns, and entablatures distinguished by continuous curves. Even excepting such extremes, during the Baroque period the taste for curves was marked, and found further expression in the frequent use of volutes, scrolls and, above all, what the Italians call *orecchioni* (literally, "ears"), ornamental elements in the form of a ribbon curling round at the ends, which were used to connect two points at different levels harmoniously. These were adopted primarily as a feature on church façades, where they were

Above
Churrigueira, main altar of the church of San Esteban, Salamanca.

Opposite right
Francesco Borromini, internal view of the cupola of Sant'Ivo alla Sapienza, Rome.

cyma

used so regularly as to be perhaps the easiest way of identifying a Baroque exterior. In spite of their bizarre shape their function was not purely decorative, but principally a strengthening, functional one. The churches of the period were almost always built with vaulted ceilings. A vault is basically a collection of arches that tend to exert an outward pressure on the supporting walls; in any vaulted building something is needed to counter this pressure. The element supplying this counter-thrust is the buttress, a typical feature of the architecture of the Middle Ages, when the difficulty was first confronted. To introduce the buttress into a Baroque construction it had to have a form compatible with that of the other parts and avoid references to the "barbaric" Gothic architecture of the past. This was a problem of some importance in an age enamored of formal consistency – and was solved by the use of scrolls. The greatest English architect of the age, Sir Christopher Wren, unable for other reasons to use the convenient scroll motif for St. Paul's Cathedral, yet having somehow to provide buttresses, made the bold decision to raise the walls of the outer aisles to the height of those of the nave so that they might act as screens, with the sole purpose of concealing the incompatible buttresses. Another, and decisive,

Guarino Guarini, Palazzo Carignano, Turin.

Movement

Baroque art was in love with movement. The curved façade, already seen in Borromini's work, became one of the distinctive features of the architecture of this period, especially in Italy. In this particular case it was combined with the traditional stress on the central part of the façade, detached from the rest of the building by curves and marked by a large doorway beneath a small portico and an elaborate cornice.

Above left
Church of San Sebastiano at Melilli, detail of a scroll.

Above right
Church of San Giorgio, Ragusa, detail of a scroll with the equestrian statue of the saint.

Left
Detail of the façade of the church of San Giuseppe in Milan, designed by Francesco Maria Richini.

Opposite page
Guarino Guarini, exterior of the dome of the chapel of the Holy Shroud, Turin. Variations on the central plan covered with a dome were a favorite feature of this architect's work. The drum is closed by the sinuous outline of the windows; above is a striking sequence of arches that reveals the internal structure; the pagoda-style top plays on gradually decreasing concentric motifs, inserted one above the other.

consequence of the vision of a building as a single mass to be articulated was that a construction was no longer seen as the sum of individual parts – façade, ground-plan, internal walls, dome, apse and so on – each one of which might be designed separately. As a result, the traditional rules that determined the planning of these parts lost importance or were totally disregarded. For example, for the architects of the Renaissance the façade of a church or a palace had been a rectangle or a series of rectangles each of which had corresponded to a story of the building. For Baroque architects the façade was merely that part of the building that faced outward, one

element of a single entity. The division into stories was generally retained, but almost always the central part of the façade was organized with more attention to what was above and below it than to what stood on either side. It was given a vertical emphasis, which strongly contrasted with the practice of horizontal division in stories. Furthermore, the elements of the façade that is those projecting from the wall surface – columns, pilasters, cornices or pediments – were grouped into the center, which thus came to dominate the sides. Although at first sight such a façade might seem to be divided horizontally, more careful observation reveals that it is organized vertically in

Search for complex form
The search for a complex form based on specific rules is taken to an extreme in the dome of San Lorenzo, with its interwoven arches.

Bottom left
Interior of the dome over the main chapel in the church of San Lorenzo, Turin.

The importance of light
Light was fundamental for Baroque architects. The strong contrasts between brightly illuminated and shadowed areas are typical of their buildings and help to create a dramatic atmosphere.

"slices," as it were. In the center is the more massive, more important section and, as the eye moves outwards, the sides appear less "heavy." The final effect is that of a building that has been shaped according to sculptural percepts, rather than put together using a traditionally architectural approach. A Baroque building is complex, surprising, and dynamic but its characteristic features are only fully comprehended if it is lit in a particular way. This requirement led to further innovations. It is not the light that falls on a particular point in a given building that varies, but the effect the light produces in striking one surface rather than another. It is obvious

Guarino Guarini, dome and interior of the church of San Lorenzo, Turin.
As well as an architect, Guarini was a mathematician and writer of treatises. He used complicated geometric figures in his works to produce fantastic results, and he was more successful than anyone else at realizing one of the concerns of Baroque art – the suggestion of an infinite dimension. In this dome the result is largely the effect of the play of light, the lower part being in shadow and the upper brightly illuminated. The undulating interior shows characteristically heavily decorated arches, a combination of sculpture and architecture that was almost the trademark of Baroque.

231

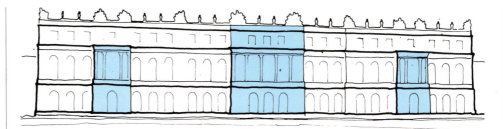

that the texture of a brick wall is not the same as that of a similar wall in smooth marble or rough-hewn stone. This fact was exploited by Baroque architects for both the exteriors and interiors of their buildings. Renaissance buildings, like many modern ones, were based on simple, elementary proportions and relationships; their significance rested in the observer's appreciation of the harmony that united the various parts of the whole. These proportions were perceptible by looking at the fabric of the building: all that was required of the light was to make them clearly visible.

The ideal effect, sought

Jules Hardouin Mansart, the front overlooking the garden, Palace of Versailles. The simple outline of this palace was conceived mainly as a backdrop for the huge gardens designed by the landscape architect André Le Nôtre. These parks, with their large lakes and long straight avenues that disappeared into the distance, were an essential feature of French country palace design.

French style

In France the Baroque style was decidedly more restrained than in Italy or Spain. Indeed, transalpine architects paved the way for a more measured, almost classical, and independent style than that which gradually emerged elsewhere in Europe. The Palace of Versailles, seen here, is perhaps one of their most accomplished examples. The garden façade has just one distinctive feature, three loggias two stories high.

With the creation of the Stupinigi Hunting Lodge, initially destined for the hunting pursuits of the court and later extended as a summer residence, Juvarra accomplished the passage from the castle to the 18th-century villa. Examination of the plan reveals the building's perfect spatial articulation, arranged around a central hall to which are added the cross-shaped blocks of Sant'Andrea and the side wings providing apartments, service areas and stables. These arms embrace, in four obtuse angles, the vast court of honor and at the same time blend harmoniously into the natural surroundings. The guiding principles behind this solution lie in the search for continuous movement and the attention to the effects of light. The construction becomes the main nucleus of the space around it, and the perspectives of the long endless avenues all start from the central hall. The interior was inspired by the theme of the garden, from plays of composition applied to the tapestries, ceilings, panels and doors, right down to the precious wooden and ivory inlay of the furniture by Pietro Piffetti.

in almost all the buildings of that period, is that produced by a monochrome, uniform lighting. Baroque replaced logic with a desire to surprise, "effect," as it would be called in the theater. As in the theater, this is achieved more easily by concentrating light on one area, leaving others in darkness or in shadow.

How is this achieved in architecture? There are various possibilities: by the juxtaposition of strong projecting elements with abrupt, deep recesses; or by breaking up the surface, making it less smooth in some way – to return, for example, to the example used earlier, by

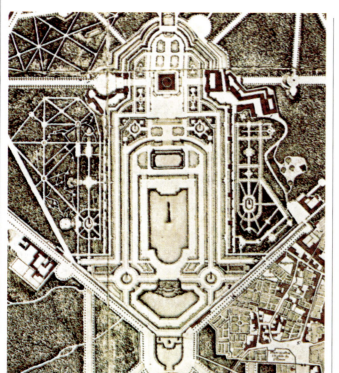

Above
Philippe Hardy, Island of Children; *Palace of Versailles.*

Left
General plan of Marly, the country residence of the king of France at the turn of the 18th century. The Baroque period also abounded with inventive designs. One of the most characteristic creations was the "French" garden which featured a number of long, straight avenues converging on circuses embellished with large lakes.

changing a marble-clad or plaster-covered wall to one of large, rough stones. Such lighting requirements had a direct influence on architectural decoration, the small-scale elements, often carved, which animate the surfaces of a building. It was in the Baroque period above all that such decoration ran riot and became distinctive, invading every corner and point where two surfaces met, where it served to conceal and maintain a sense of continuity. The "Undulating" order was added to the five traditional orders of architecture – Tuscan, Doric, Ionic, Corinthian, and Composite. Another new and popular variant was the "Giant order," running up through two or three stories. The details of the traditional orders were enriched and made more complex: entablatures had greater projection and details sometimes become almost capricious. The arches connecting one column or pilaster to the next were no longer restricted to a semicircle but were often elliptical or oval. They took the form, unique to the Baroque, of a double curve: describing a curve, that is, not only when seen from the front but also when seen from above. Sometimes arches were broken with straight sections inserted into the curve. This

View of the Reggia di Caserta and a detail of the gardens.
Charles de Bourbon asked Luigi Vanvitelli to construct this palace in 1751. Here the garden is the venue for sculpted theatrical scenes inspired by classical mythology. The route encounters the myths of Diana and Actaeon, Ceres, Juno, and Aeolus along a sort of river path created by water from the Carolino Aqueduct.

characteristic feature was also used in pediments, above a door, a window, or a whole building. The standard shape of the pediment had been either triangular or semicircular. In the Baroque period, however, it was sometimes broken (as if split and slipped upwards) or combined curved and straight lines; or fanciful, as for example in Guarino Guarini's scheme for Palazzo Carignano, where they appeared around doors and windows like curtains drawn back. Windows too were often far removed from the classical forms; added to rectangular or square shapes, sometimes with rounded tops, typical of the Renaissance; instead oval or square ones were topped by a segment of a circle, or rectangles were placed beneath little oval windows. Other details appeared on entablatures, doors, the keystones of arches and corners, everywhere: volutes, stucco figures, huge, complex, and majestic scrolls and all sorts of fantastic and grotesque shapes. One characteristic and striking form of decoration was the use of the tower, sometimes single, sometimes in pairs, but always complex and highly decorated, erected on the façade, and sometimes on the domes of

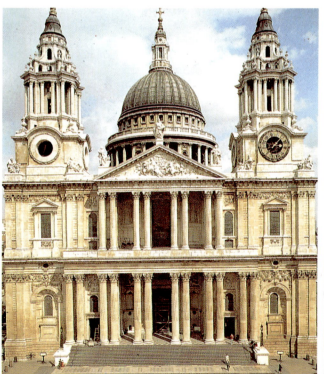

Above
William Kent, Chiswick House. This is the most characteristic achievement of English Neo-Palladianism and presents a square plan with rooms distributed organically around a central room. Despite the measured proportions, the façade is made monumental by the portico, steps and dome above with its large thermal windows.

Left
Christopher Wren, St. Paul's Cathedral in London (1675-1710).

churches. In some countries, in particular Austria, Germany, and Spain, this was used so often as to become the norm. These were the most obvious and frequently used motifs of Baroque architecture, although each country developed these elements in different ways and an understanding of these regional and national differences is essential to a proper understanding of the Baroque as a whole.

Italy, the cradle of Baroque, in addition to a considerable number of good professional architects, produced four excellent ones: Gian Lorenzo Bernini, Borromini, Pietro da Cortona, and Guarino Guarini. The work of each was unmistakably Baroque, but each had his own style. Bernini and, to a lesser extent Pietro da Cortona, represented the courtly Baroque, majestic and exuberant but never outrageously so and successful principally in Italy. This style comprised all the features of Baroque described above and conveyed an air of grandeur and dignity that rendered it almost a "classic" of its kind. Borromini's designs were quite different, far more tortured, intellectual, and original. Each of Bernini's architectural works was marked by some ingenious idea that provided the starting point: the great ellipse of the piazza in front of St.

German-speaking countries
Johann Lukas von Hildebrandt, the Upper Belvedere, Vienna. The Baroque style of Austria and Germany was inspired by both French and Italian examples. The Upper Belvedere, built for Prince Eugene of Savoy, is distinctly Baroque in its pomp but restrained with a well-balanced distribution of volumes.

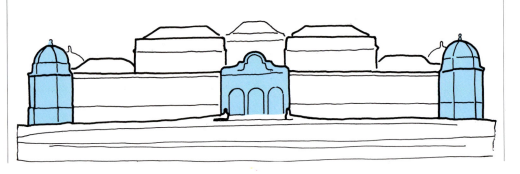

Filippo Juvarra, Palazzo Madama, Turin (1718-1721).

Johann Bernhard Fischer, the Schönbrunn Palace in Vienna. This is a more accomplished composition than Versailles; the façade shows the typical Baroque emphasis on the center and the use here of an order three stories high is more in keeping with the size of the building.

Peter's in Rome, or the little round portico on the front of Sant'Andrea al Quirinale. Typical of Borromini were extremely complex ground plans and masonry, and the deliberate contradiction of traditional detail – the inversion of volutes, for instance, or entablatures that no longer rested on capitals but on an extension of them and so on. Many of his ideas were adopted by Guarini, who added a mathematical and technical component that was of great importance both in itself and for its

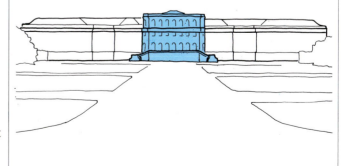

237

influence on Baroque architects outside Italy, especially in Germany. Personal variations apart, Italian Baroque could be said to correspond almost completely to the canons described. The same cannot be said of France, which produced a number of excellent architects, perhaps more than Italy: Salomon de Brosse, François Mansart, Louis Le Vau, Jacques Lemercier, and, greatest of all, Jules Hardouin Mansart. In France personality was less significant than the school to which architects could be said to belong. The attempt of the French court to introduce Italian Baroque into France by summoning Bernini in 1665 to Paris and commissioning him to redesign the royal palace – the Louvre – was doomed from the outset. As one critic rightly

Johann Bernhard Fischer von Erlach, Karlskirche, Vienna.
The design of a church with a central dome flanked by two side towers, already a feature of Italian Baroque, was particularly popular in Austria and other German-speaking countries, where it practically became the norm for church façades. In the Karlskirche, the architect has added two pillars modeled on Trajan's column in Rome between the central block and the towers.

Side towers
In functional terms the two side towers are superfluous but their presence transforms a centralized design, dominated by a dome, into a pyramid with the roofs of the towers balancing that of the dome.

Jacob Prandtauer, Melk Convent, Austria.
The imposing and complex spatial organization of Baroque architecture is clearly visible at Melk. The church, the termination of the long convent building behind it, overlooks a forecourt entered through the large serliana set beneath a terrace (to the fore). Again the façade design is based on two side towers, although they are taller and closer together than usual.

Right
Kilian Ignaz Dientzenhofer, church of St. John, Prague.
In this building perfect harmony has been attained between the plan and the external structures, as seen in the unusual diagonal position of the bell towers. This solution reconciles the desire for a harmoniously organized plan and the search for a scenographic façade.

Left

Pedro de Ribeira, doorway of the San Fernando hospice in Madrid.

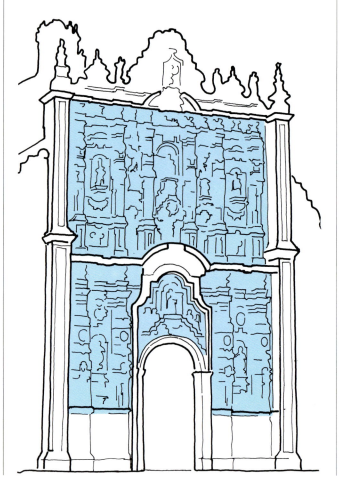

Below

Lorenzo Rodriguez, chapel, Mexico City.

The Baroque style spread from Spain and Portugal to their colonies in Latin America and if possible was further enriched. Buildings were encrusted with elaborate ornament becoming more reminiscent of fine metalwork – hence the name "plateresque," after plata or silver. This style was used in architectural decoration.

observed, a radical difference of temperament was involved. To the French, Italian exuberance verged on the indecorous, if not willful, and was in bad taste. Rather than artists, French architects considered themselves professional men, dedicated to the service and glorification of their king. At the court of the Sun King the Baroque style developed was more restrained than the Italian: ground-plans were less complex, and façades more severe, with greater respect for

Baroque art in Spain
In Spain Baroque appeared as trite and decorated as its French counterpart was restrained and imposing. It was called "churriguerisque" after the Churrigueras, a family of architects that covered Spanish buildings with layers of exuberant decoration. Santiago de Compostela is a typical example with its mass of spires, pinnacles and statues.

Fernando Casas y Novoa, cathedral of Santiago de Compostela, Spain.
The façade enclosed by two bell towers shows the dense sculptural decoration that was typical of Spanish Baroque.

the details and proportions of the traditional architectural orders, with no violent effects or flagrant whims. The textbook example and greatest achievement of French Baroque is the chateau of Versailles, the royal palace built for Louis XIV outside Paris: a huge U-shaped block with two long wings, only slightly disturbed by the small, low arcades on the main façade overlooking the gardens. The great glory of

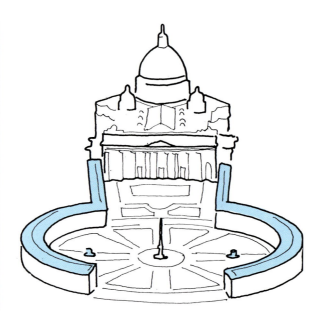

Town planning

Baroque architecture was not concerned with buildings alone and extended its interest to new fields: roads, squares, and gardens; in other words, what today is known as town planning. This evolution was congenial to the highly theatrical spirit of the times and the Baroque masters possessed the technical skills to resolve the new, complex themes.

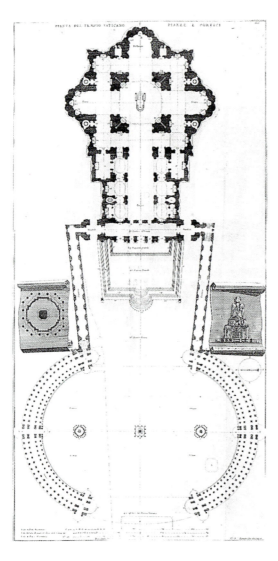

Plan of the basilica and colonnade of St. Peter's in the Vatican.
In 1656 Pope Alexander VII decided to alter the large area in front of the church and called upon Bernini to resolve the problems which conditioned the final choice. The new square had to satisfy the need for monumentality but at the same time correct the problem of an excessively horizontal façade and connect the church visually to the Papal palace, from which the pope normally blessed pilgrims. The oval plan and Doric porticoes enclosing the square between two grandiose semicircles reflect a new concept of space but, at the same time, do resolve all the problems posed.

St. Peter's Square in Rome, by Gian Lorenzo Bernini, is the best-known example of Baroque town planning. It comprises a large oval colonnade linked to the church by two slanting wings. The effect is solemn but welcoming, the two huge stone arms expressing the Catholic church's ecumenical mission to "embrace" the whole world. It is significant that Baroque was originally the architecture of the Counter-Reformation.

French Baroque was to be found not in architecture but in the art of landscape gardening. Until the Baroque era gardens had been of the "Italian" type, small parks with plants and flowerbeds laid out in geometrical or architectural schemes. André Le Nôtre, the brilliant landscape architect who created a new style of garden, supplanted these with the "French" garden, of which the park at Versailles was to become both prototype and masterpiece. In the center stood the palace; on one side was the drive, the gates, the wide graveled area for carriages; and on the other were lawns and parterres, flowerbeds in geometrical shapes, fountains, canals and broad expanses of water and, beyond this, the dark line of woods pierced by long, wide, straight avenues linked to each other by circular clearings.

The imposing and austere architecture created in France, with its balance of Baroque trends and classical traditions, was gradually to become the most advanced cultural model in Europe. When Sir Christopher Wren, in the second half of the 17th century, decided to update his ideas, he went not to Italy, as had previously been the

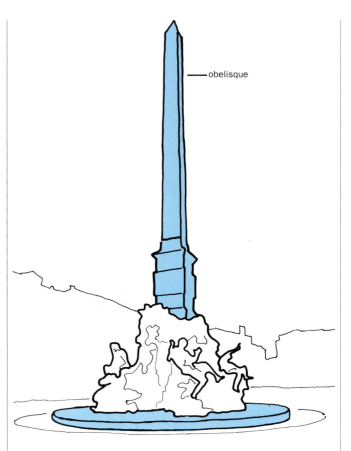

obelisque

Fusion of the arts

The fusion of the different arts is characteristic of the Baroque period. This example shows how sculpture is assigned a role in town planning. The Fontana dei Fiumi occupies the center of the Piazza Navona and constitutes its focal point. The upper part of the fountain is a monument – an Egyptian obelisque. The main portion is a grand ensemble of sculpture with gigantic personages representing the rivers. It is this lower portion – alive with movement and water – that reveals the spirit of the work. Such a combination of forms, methods and meanings is typical of the period.

custom, but to Paris. The Baroque architecture of Belgium and the Netherlands also bears the mark of French inspiration.

Closer to the Italian model was the Baroque seen north of the Alps, in Austria and Germany. This was the case, however, only in a restricted sense. Baroque influence came relatively late to the German states, devastated in the first half of the 17th century by the Thirty Years War. Once acclimatized, however, it grew remarkably both in quantity and quality. The great architects of the period practiced at a relatively late time, at the end of the 17th and the

Gian Lorenzo Bernini and assistants, the Fontana dei Fiumi, Rome.

The fountain – its sculptural aspect and construction, its movement, in part, and its insertion into an urban framework – is a key theme in Baroque art. Contrary to its former treatment, it stands alone, although it relates to the buildings and spaces around it. The sculptures are of fundamental importance (see details on this and the opposite pages). They are typically Baroque in the play of swollen muscles, curly hair and beards, and agitated poses.

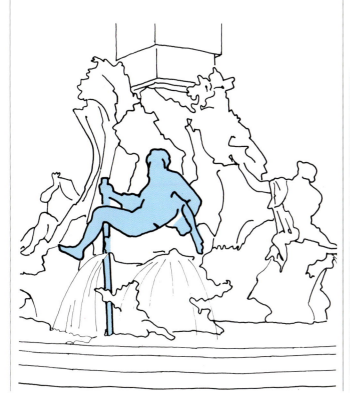

beginning of the 18th centuries. They were, however, numerous, exceptionally gifted, and blessed with enthusiastic patronage from the several royal, ducal, and episcopal courts of Germany. All visited Rome and were trained in the Italian tradition: Johann Bernhard Fischer von Erlach – the most famous and perhaps the greatest –, Johann Lukas von Hildebrandt and Johann Balthasar Neumann, his probably more gifted pupil; to these must be added Matthäus Pöppelmann,

Above
Luigi Vanvitelli, staircase inside the Reggia di Caserta.

Left
Balthasar Neumann, staircase in the Würzburg palace.
Intended as the most distinctive part of the residence, this is certainly one of the grandest examples of German Baroque architecture. The large rectangular hall contains a straight staircase set away from the walls which, at the landing turns at an angle of 180° to divide into two parallel flights. The articulated space generated provides a number of unexpected viewpoints and intersecting perspectives, from the farthest corner of the atrium to the airy vaulted ceiling.

The importance of the staircase
In the Baroque period the staircase became one of the main focal points of a building. Many types were invented, including the "imperial staircase" – a single flight which then divides into two side ones. This one is in Palazzo Madama, Turin, and starts from a single point then turns back on two sides to join again above the entrance.

François de Cuvilliés – a Frenchman who was active almost exclusively in Germany. The Baroque style created by these men was to spread to Poland, the Baltic states, and eventually to Russia. It had considerable affinity with Italian Baroque, but with an even greater tendency towards exuberant decoration, especially of the interior; it also differed from Italian forms in its avoidance of sharp contrasts of light and shade in favor of more diffused and serene luminosity. These characteristics also anticipated the Rococo style that was to succeed it, a style that found its widest application in these countries and was sometimes the work of the same architects, for example Pöppelmann, Neumann, and Cuvilliés. In the two main building types, churches and palaces, the Baroque of the German-speaking countries adhered consistently to a few basic designs. In churches the two lateral towers with which Borromini already had experimented were adopted systematically.

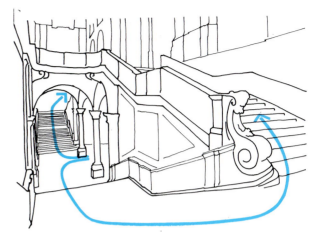

Filippo Juvarra, staircase in Palazzo Madama, Turin. Baroque artists loved movement and scenographic effect; it was a supremely theatrical period. What element could be more fittingly suited to this than grand staircases in palace entrances? As a result, the Baroque taste for complicated plans and ostentations and animated designs was used to create imposing architectural "machines."

Sometimes this was taken to the point of upsetting the general layout, as Fischer von Erlach did in Vienna on his Karlskirche. On this, a centrally planned building, he added the towers as freestanding, voided structures on either side of the main body of the church. The whole edifice exemplifies a theatrical conception in the grand style, its form emphasized by two columns, reminiscent of Trajan's Column in Rome, which stand beside the towers. In palace design the model was Versailles, but German and Austrian architects generally proved better in the articulation of large masses of masonry, accentuating the central

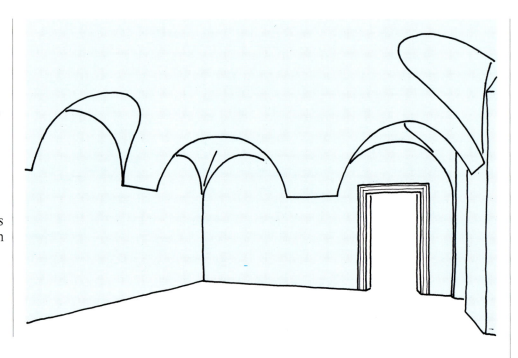

and sometimes the lateral sections of the building. At the same time that its influence was spreading north of the Alps, Italian Baroque was also

asserting itself in Spain and Portugal. In these countries there was no obstacle to its success, but an entirely individual style developed. Its

primary – indeed its only real – characteristic was profuse decoration. Whatever its form, a building seemed merely to serve as a pretext for

Painted architecture

One widespread feature of Baroque palaces – in all the countries it influenced – is the salon, painted with architecture and landscapes that seem to extend the real architecture into infinity. In extreme examples such as this, the "true" architecture is little more than a box enriched with a myriad of illusionistic effects and painted scenes.

Left
The Hall of Perspectives, Stupinigi Hunting Lodge.

Opposite page
The Belvedere Palace, Vienna.
A concern with the fusion of the various arts, a love of make-believe and a desire to suggest boundless space – all these typical characteristics of Baroque found their application in painted rooms. The painting could be illusionistic, that is simulate reality, or decorative and abstract, but it always conditioned the overall perception of space.

ornamentation. Many factors contributed to this result, the principal ones being the Moorish tradition, still alive on the Iberian peninsula, and the influences of pre-Columbian American art, with its fantastic decorative vocabulary. This particular style, known as "churrigueresque" after the family name, Churriguera, of a dynasty of Spanish architects who were particularly closely associated with it, dominated Spain and Portugal for two centuries and was taken to the South American colonies, where the decoration was, if anything, intensified to a frenzy of ornamentation. Its value is perhaps debatable, but as a style it is certainly recognizable, in its subordination of everything to decoration. A number of more general themes were also typical of the Baroque style of architecture. The first was the way in which Baroque architects were the first to confront the task of town planning practically rather than in theory. Principally, they dealt with it in terms of a rotary and avenues. Into the fabric of the city they

Below

The Equerry Room, with paintings by Amedeo Cignaroli, Stupinigi Hunting Lodge. A reflection of the refined requests of Charles Emmanuel III and his consort, the interior of this palace adheres to the models of European courts. *Juvarra's careful attention to the constant exchanges between architecture and the minor arts and the presence of highly skilled workers have here produced surprising results.*

cut circular plazas, each dominated by some structure, a church, a palace, a fountain, and then linked these points with a network of long, straight avenues. It was not a perfect solution, but it was ingenious. Indeed, for the first time a system was devised for planning, or replanning, a city, making it more beautiful, more theatrical, and above all more comprehensible by subordinating it to a rule. The use of such schemes for town planning, which parallel those of the French garden, conceived on the same principle, brought with it a fashion for monumental fountains, in which architecture, sculpture and water were combined to form an ideal centerpiece and express the Baroque feeling for scenography and movement. It is no accident that Rome, the city that more than any other was replanned to the new norms of the 17th century, is *the* city of fountains. Two other characteristic themes of Baroque style are found

Galleries

Along with staircases, the most characteristic invention of Baroque architecture was the gallery, a wide covered corridor between rooms which often became an elegant space in its own right. Usually covered with a vaulted ceiling, opening outward on one side and onto rooms on the other, it was often embellished with frescoes and mirrors.

Above
The marble gallery in the Lower Belvedere, Vienna.

Left
Cabinet from France; London, Victoria and Albert Museum.

Jules Hardouin Mansart, Galerie des Glaces, Palace of Versailles.
The gallery was not just a place of passage but, at least initially, also used for display purposes, as in this famous example created by closing the original loggia. Galleries were often used to house paintings and other works of art – hence the name given now – to space used to display this type of collection.

in building interiors: great complex staircases began to appear in all aristocratic buildings from the 17th century onward, sometimes becoming the dominating feature and the gallery, in origin a wide, richly decorated corridor, another showpiece, of which the Galerie des Glaces at Versailles is an outstanding example. As time progressed these galleries were used to house the family treasures (paintings, sculptures, and curios) and this led to today's application of the word to an art collection. Often the gallery, like many other rooms in the Baroque period, would be painted with illusionistic scenes, which often intruded on the architecture, reducing it to a secondary role. This is another example of the Baroque taste for the overlapping of art forms, and the point at which architecture yields to painting.

Left

A royal prie-dieu from Italy; Florence, Palazzo Pitti. Made for the Grand Duke of Tuscany, Cosimo de'Medici, this is a typically 17th century Florentine composition, clearly influenced by architecture. This is visible in the tiered bands on the base, the presence of Tuscan-order columns and a broken tympanum with contrasting volutes which crown this sumptuous, grave and austere piece.

"Wonder"

The use of statues of female figures – caryatids – or male ones – telamons – to support a roof is an ancient one but became particularly popular during the Baroque, being extremely suited to the taste for the unusual, obviously absurd and surprise effect. This model found great favor in Austrian buildings, to which this famous example belongs.

Johann Lukas von Hildebrandt, interior of the Belvedere Palace, Vienna. Baroque characteristically gave its sculpture architectural functions. This case also features an apparent paradox – because it seems incredible or impossible that the statues can physically sustain the load placed on them. Surprise is mingled with wonder, the maximum requirement of the Baroque style.

Staircase, Upper Belvedere, decorated with sculptures and reliefs depicting the life of Alexander the Great.

253

PAINTING

It is appropriate to begin an account of Baroque painting with its favorite genre: the illusionistic decoration of the walls of an interior. Obviously the idea of using a wall to display a painted scene was as old as art; what was new, or almost new, was the use made of this technique by Baroque artists. On the walls, and more especially on the ceilings, of churches and palaces they painted vast, animated scenes, which tend to produce in the spectator the impression that the wall or ceiling no longer exists, or at least that they open it out in a striking manner. This, again, was not really new, but in the Baroque period it became almost an absolute rule, combining as it did all the aesthetic features of the time: grandeur, theatricality, movement, the representation of infinity, and in addition almost superhuman technical skill.

It showed that tendency to combine the various forms of art for a unified effect, which was the most distinctive characteristic of the age. In the best examples of illusionistic decoration it is hard to say where the architecture ends and the painting begins. Such illusionistic paintings varied greatly in the stories they told – lives of saints, kings, heroes, mythical figures – but they were consistent in the elements they employed: architectural glories standing out against the sky; soaring angels and saints; figures in swift motion, their garments billowing out in the wind; all depicted with bold foreshortening – the perspective effect of looking upward from below or conversely downward from above, which makes the figures appear shorter. Such was the vitality of the genre that it continued not only throughout the 17th

Illusionistic perspective
Andrea Pozzo, Glorification of St. Ignatius; *Rome, church of Sant'Ignazio. During the Baroque period the application of illusionistic painting based on perspective was much in vogue. It was a distinctive feature used to cover the ceilings of churches and palaces with bold architecture and boundless spaces. This trend contained all the characteristic features of Baroque: grandiose effect, movement, technical skill, and illusion.*

century but well into the 18th, extending into what is generally considered the age of Rococo. With the passing of time only the general atmosphere of the paintings changed. Dark, dramatic and violent initially, they gradually became brighter, more vivid, and lively. This was partly due to changing fashions and partly because the leading artists of the genre were nearly all of Venetian origin and training, bound to a tradition of color more

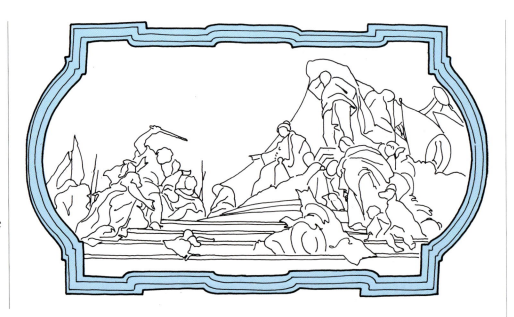

Architectural frames

Illusionistic painting within architectural frames was a characteristic of the Baroque. Its evolution ended with the work of Tiepolo, well into the 18th century. This master also adopted new patterns, including the "centrifugal" composition, the placing of the figures to the sides leaving a wide area of sky in the middle.

Left
Jacob Jordaens, The Four Evangelists; Paris, Musée du Louvre.
There are still doubts about the subject of this painting which may portray the young Christ explaining the scriptures to the doctors. Jordaens' energic plastic vision is condensed in the close-set group of figures that fills the entire surface.

pleasing than the Roman and indeed Italian school in general. Naturally, painting was not confined to the walls of buildings. There was also, and indeed especially, a tradition of painting on canvas, and as with architecture the characteristics of the various national schools differed widely. They had one concern in common, however: the study of light and its effects.

The impulse came from Italy, indeed from a single Italian artist, Michelangelo

Giambattista Tiepolo,
Judgment of Solomon, *the*
whole and detail; Udine,
Arcivescovado.
The figures stand
out clearly against the
brightly lit heavens.
All are foreshortened by the
finest perspective
techniques
and are fixed in great,
grandiose gestures,
seemingly inspired by
theatrical mime.

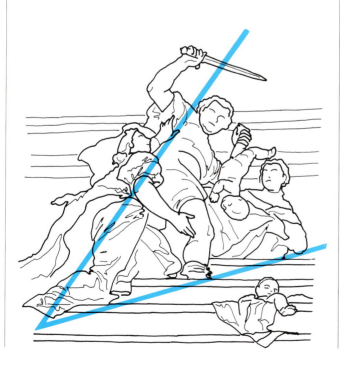

DEATH AND VANITAS IN 17TH-CENTURY ART

Looming above 17th-century devotion were the incessant Biblical references to the transience of life and material assets, summed up in the famous verse of Ecclesiastes 1.2: *Vanitas vanitatum, omnia vanitas* ("Vanity of vanities! All is vanity"). This is a typical cry of counter-reformation piety. In his *Spiritual Exercises* St. Ignatius recommended meditation on death, and Jesuit literature had subsequently developed the theme with an insistence destined to instill anxiety in the believer about his destiny and desire for repentance. Emile Mâle duly linked the significance of gloomy motifs and macabre symbols – as if in a revival of medieval fears – for 17th-century art to the propagation of these texts. From the end of the previous century, the idea of death dominated the systems created for the formal celebration of funerals or masses offered for the souls. "In Rome, in 1572, the funeral of Sigismund II, king of Poland, was held in the church of San Lorenzo in Damaso. The catafalque, covered with hundreds of candles, looked like a staircase of fire, a tall pyramid; on the top, the huge eagle of Poland appeared to have just landed, its great wings outspread. Funeral drapes adorned the church and skeletons stood out against the black background, some brandishing scythes, other signaling mysteriously to those present. Seated immobile beside the catafalque were monks, their hoods drawn over their eyes, like apparitions." The transience of time and the inevitability of death are great themes of 17th-century morality. The combination of the hourglass and the skull returns, for instance, in a severe *Still Life* by Philippe de Champaigne in Le Mans Museum (below), the moral meaning being stressed by the inclusion of a cut tulip, destined to wither quickly, like the life of man.

Merisi, known as Caravaggio after the town where he was born. Although his work was more attacked than appreciated by his contemporaries he undoubtedly marked the beginning of a new era. At the time of Caravaggio, painting had fully attained the objective set two centuries earlier: the faithful representation of nature in all its manifestations. A new line of study was required and this Caravaggio supplied. His paintings showed sturdy peasants, innkeepers, and gamblers, though they might sometimes be dressed as saints, apostles, and fathers of the Church. This was in itself a break with the Renaissance, with its aristocratic figures and idealized surroundings. The most important aspect of Baroque painting was not however *what* was represented but *how* it was represented. The painting was not lit uniformly but

in patches; details struck by bright, intense light alternated with areas of dark shadow. It was a dramatic, violent style of painting, eminently suited to an age of strong aesthetic contrasts, as the Baroque period was. Yet the essential aspects of Baroque painting developed very little in Italy, which produced a large number of decorators who continued the tradition of illusionistic painting into the late 17th century but no painters worthy of following in Caravaggio's footsteps. His legacy was taken up in Spain, in Flanders, and Holland. There, unlike architecture, painting had developed flourishing local

Contrasts of light and shade

Light, or the rendering of the effects it creates, is a distinctive feature of Baroque painting. The first to make a decisive step in this direction was Caravaggio, whose work influenced all the art of the period. In his paintings, light only illuminates certain areas, the most significant. The rest remains in shadow, providing a violent and characteristic contrast.

Left
Michelangelo Merisi, known as Caravaggio, Head of Medusa; Florence, Uffizi.

schools that were to the fore in artistic exploration. Flemish painters had created a genre of painting concerned with the faithful representation of domestic life and everyday reality that had no parallels in Italy – where there was indeed no demand for such pictures. The Flemish painters had exported to Italy the technique of oil painting, formerly unknown to the artists of the early Italian Renaissance.
This development had different results in Flanders and the Netherlands respectively and was associated with the two profoundly different personalities of Rubens and Rembrandt.

Michelangelo Merisi, known as Caravaggio, Martyrdom of St. Matthew; *Rome, church of San Luigi dei Francesi.*
Caravaggio's works alternate brightly illuminated areas with dark shadows, contrasts that lend a striking emphasis to the figures, rendered with great realism. His painting is "explosive," the epitome of the Baroque style.

Right
Michelangelo Merisi, known as Caravaggio, Bowl of Fruit; *Milan, Pinacoteca Ambrosiana.*

Peter Paul Rubens's work was vigorous, confident, sensual, decorative, theatrical, and energetically magnificent. In fact, when Rubens, a promising painter from Antwerp, arrived to study in Italy – where he remained for eight years – he focused mainly on the Venetians. When he returned to his native city he opened a workshop where he was soon employing two hundred assistants, many of whom were outstanding painters, each with his own specialty: the painting of animals, of fabrics, of still life, and so on. He himself specialized in the human body – which he depicted with an abundance of rosy flesh – with broad, strong gestures, and a continuous play of curves, each one drawing the eye to another, the sum of which determined the general outline of the painting – a lozenge, a circle, an S, and so on. These robust figures, which move as expansively as though they were on a stage constitute the most immediately recognizable characteristic of his art, an art that is joyous, robust, and almost unbelievably prolific. All Flemish painting was influenced by this prodigious artistic patriarch but no one came close to rivaling the master; some devoted

themselves to one or another aspect of his work. The most famous of Rubens's pupils, Anthony van Dyck, specialized in portraits, in which he attained his greatest successes. Both in the general composition of these paintings and in the poses of their subjects he was far more restrained than his master and his coloring was more subdued. The subject was portrayed in a moment of repose, or at least of calm; the pose was dignified; the background was always mannered, such as an unidentified landscape, or the plinth of a column. As the court painter of Charles I, van Dyck was the founder of an English school of portrait painting. Rubens personified the exuberant, theatrical, courtly side of Baroque art. Rembrandt, on the other hand, the greatest painter of the Netherlands, represented its tormented, dramatic, introverted

Peter Paul Rubens, Rape of the Daughters of Leucippus; *Munich, Alte Pinakothek. Rubens studied for eight years in Italy, particularly admiring Venetian painters, because to his mind, color was the most important factor, combined with sensual vigor.*

263

aspect. He was Caravaggio's heir. Rembrandt was not an isolated phenomenon and his work formed part of a collective enterprise. The United Provinces, of which Holland was one, were the northern part of the Low Countries, less developed than Flanders and once perhaps the "poor relations" of the Flemish. But the long struggle fought against the greatest power of the time, Spain, in the name of independence and religious freedom had reawakened the people. In the 17th century the nation was rich, proud and expanding in influence. It was also addicted to painting; every sort of person indulged it

in some way: merchants, the middle classes, craftsmen, sailors – all knew or claimed to know something about it. The paintings they wanted and which they commissioned from their artists were, however, different from Italian paintings, even from those of Rubens. Being Protestants, the Dutch had banished religious painting, which was almost the only kind known in Catholic countries. Once they had gained their independence, they expressed their contentment in the enjoyment of the good things of life: fine, solid houses; convivial company; clothes of high quality. They were, in

short, bourgeois, and they wanted bourgeois paintings: scenes of everyday life to hang in ordinary houses and so painted on small canvases. For these reasons Holland seemed the least likely country to receive a transplantation of the violent, tormented art of Caravaggio. Indeed, a typical Dutch painter was Frans Hals, who specialized in the subjects most in demand: individual and group portraits. The latter were characteristic of the country and the time. During the war with Spain, many companies of volunteer soldiers had been formed. After the Dutch victory their members had not

Anthony van Dyck, Sir Endimion Porter and Anthony van Dyck*; Madrid, Prado.*

Refined worldliness

Van Dyck was a pupil of Rubens and absorbed some of his characteristics, specializing in portraits of distinctive refinement and restrained content. Typical of the period is the way in which light and shadows highlight the most important areas of the painting: in this case, the sovereign's face and the white coat of the horse.

Above
Anthony van Dyck, Portrait of Charles I of England; *Madrid, Prado.*
Although the model for van Dyck's works is nearly always Renaissance, the way he uses colors and illuminates the figures is characteristic of his time, here showing the worldly, courteous and refined side of its aristocracy.

Left
Anthony van Dyck, Venus in the Forge of Vulcan; *Vienna, Kunsthistorishces Museum.*

dispersed but continued to meet and each of these companies wanted a group portrait to show their members gathered together. Usually these canvases were of greater width than height, and showed the officers of the company grouped around a table or some other object that would serve as a pretext for a gathering of so many men. The lighting was depicted as natural, without any dramatic contrasts. This type of painting resolved brilliantly the two problems posed by similar portraits: how to give more or less the same importance to each person and how to avoid poses that were over-affected or theatrical and would have seemed ridiculous for

ordinary men in what was, after all, just a "group photograph." Rembrandt Harmenszoon van Rijn – his full name – also painted group portraits of this kind, but in an entirely different spirit. The most famous of these has earned the title of *The Night Watch* because of the dark background from which its figures emerge partially or wholly illuminated by patches of light; but it is not a night scene. It is a case of the application of Caravaggio's style to Dutch painting by contrasting dark shadow with areas of strong light. The traditional scheme of the group portrait is altered in another way, even more significant than the change of atmosphere. The officers do not all have

Psychological exploration
Rembrandt was a painter of such character and greatness that only convention restricts him to the label of a "Baroque artist." In his work he developed – and took to the extreme – the most Baroque of all artistic themes: that of the exploration of a situation or a character using contrasts of light and shadow around him, introducing an interest in the "moral" as well as physical portrait of the model.

Left
Rembrandt, The Night Watch, *detail;* Amsterdam, Rijksmuseum.

the same importance but are presented in strictly hierarchical order. The captain of the company and his lieutenant are seen in strong light in the center with the others around them, only their heads emerging from the shadow. This approach marked the beginning of an interest in the use of light to observe a single figure, or sometimes only a face. Rembrandt's single portraits also feature the strong contrasts of Caravaggio and indeed the shadows are even darker and invade almost the entire canvas. The light falls from one side of the subject, illuminates his face or part of it, and dramatizes every wrinkle. Sometimes it also strikes a secondary subject – a book, a table, or other object. The rest is an area of darkness. This style of painting can be called Baroque because it belongs to the 17th century, but in almost every other respect it has left behind the conventions of the period, preserving only the use of light in the composition to make the subject stand out. Spanish Baroque painting also took inspiration from Caravaggio's use of light, and the ranks of its artists numbered several masters of genre painting and of religious scenes, for example, Bartolomé Esteban Murillo; it also included such outstanding interpreters of the asceticism and spirituality of Spanish culture as Francisco de Zurbarán. But in the work of Diego

Above
Rembrandt, Self-portrait as St. Paul; Amsterdam, Rijksmuseum.
The conception of this painting is consistent with Caravaggio, but here the shadows are even gloomier and the light less bright.

Right
Rembrandt, The Anatomy Lesson; The Hague, Mauritshuis.
The portrait is here turned into an almost dramatic scene, focused on the actions of the doctor and the reactions of the onlookers. The effect is heightened by the light projected on the faces against a background in shadow.

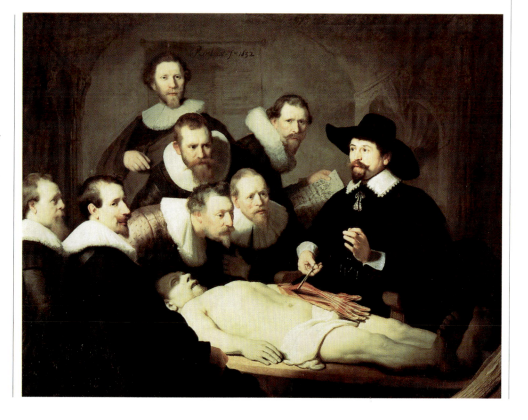

Rodriguez de Silva y Velázquez, one of the greatest painters of all times, it reached a climax. For Velázquez, Caravaggio's work was only a starting-point. In his paintings light is manipulated to reconstruct an optical realism using the effects of different tones: a reproduction of reality not faithful to the hairs of a beard or the texture of a fabric as sought by the painters of the Renaissance, but to what the eye actually sees, the general impression received when looking at something. In Velázquez's paintings light is used as painters of two centuries earlier had used perspective, to make space tangible. Areas of light and shadow are alternated to

The Dutch group portrait
Above
Frans Hals, The Governors of St. Elizabeth's Almshouses, *Haarlem; Haarlem, Frans Halsmuseum.*
Hals was the greatest interpreter of works of this kind, typical of the 17th-century Dutch group portrait genre; a background in shadow, horizontal development of the canvas and various figures grouped around a table, all more or less of the same rank. The carefully portrayed figures are lit in a uniform manner on the face, highlighted by the large, wide collars in fashion at the time.

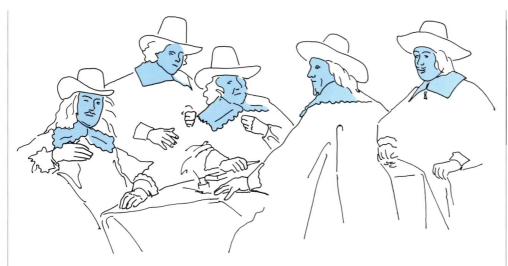

create the illusion of a place in which the figures are not painted but actually "are." These figures are painted with broad, supple strokes of the brush to delineate them clearly without going into realistic detail. The same technique was to be used in the 19th century by the French Impressionists. Not surprisingly, like them, Velázquez seemed indifferent to the "content" of what he was painting, to the great religious themes, for example, which had such importance for his contemporaries. Instead, his whole attention was concentrated on painting, on his craft. This attitude was no longer Baroque, although appearing in that period, as did a genre of painting that was to remain

Opposite page
Below left
Jan Vermeer, The Milk Woman*; Amsterdam, Rijksmuseum.*

Opposite page
Bottom right
Pieter de Hooch, The Mother*; Berlin, Staatliche Museen Preussischer Kulturbesitz.*

Below
Bartolomé Esteban Murillo, Young Drinker*; London, National Gallery.*
In contrast with the formality of the state, Spanish painting is exuberant and rich, with light always being used to stress the main features.

269

REMBRANDT'S SKETCHES

The naturalistic aspirations that characterize the work of Rembrandt led him to make many sketches, to use the immediacy of sketching to fix every aspect of reality that aroused his curiosity or caught his attention. He then defined the process of structural and chromatic clarification of his paintings in drawings and preparatory studies. The collection of drawings that the artist left after his death is truly imposing, something like 1500 in number.

These range from simple pen and ink sketches – drawn in a fast, scratching hand – to more complex sanguine, watercolor or mixed works, in which the images gradually take shape in an increasingly attentive definition of spatial, luminous and chromatic effects. Driven at every stage of his fluctuating career by the tenacious desire to capture and portray the truest reality, he penetrated the secret places of the heart, illuminating the short-lived lives of a company of unforgettable characters with supernatural light.

successful up to the present day: "still life," a picture of an arrangement of flowers or objects of one kind or another, generally painted in the studio. Of course paintings of this kind had certainly been made earlier, but now they constituted a true genre, with representatives in every country and in every school of painting. Again the artist who popularized this genre of painting was Caravaggio, who began his artistic career with this type of work. However, the genre reached its highest development in Flanders and the Netherlands, where there was already a precedent, if not a

Contrasting color
Diego Rodríguez de Silva y Velázquez, Portrait of Prince Philip Prosper*; Vienna, Kunsthistorisches Museum. Typically Baroque is the use of light in this painting – not with harsh contrasts but a continuous, gradual shifting of intensity over various parts of the canvas – to make the composition a play of symbolic color references, concealed behind an apparently total adherence to the subject. The repetition of color in the dog and child's clothes is one obvious example.*

Velázquez, Portrait of the Infanta Margarita; *Madrid, Prado.*
Nothing could be more blatantly Baroque than the full precious dress in which the princess appears engulfed. The pomp is rendered with equal grandeur by the painter who not only illuminates and highlights the colors of the dress but also repeats them in large curtains that balance the central patch of color. This is very different from the work of Caravaggio, Rubens, and Rembrandt but it is also obtained with the use of light.

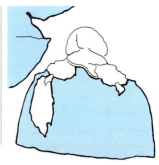

Still life

Francisco de Zurbarán, still life detail from The Portrait of Fra' Gonzalo de Ilesacs; *Guadelupe, Spain, Hieronymite Monastery. With the Baroque period a new genre of painting was added to the traditional ones, still life. This consists of an arrangement of everyday objects: flowers, fruit, books, game and so on. It is a "studio" painting, executed indoors, in which the detailed rendering of the subject using light and shadow finds its maximum field of application. Sometimes, as in this case, there is also a macabre detail, of religious inspiration, which is one of the minor but most significant features of the Baroque period.*

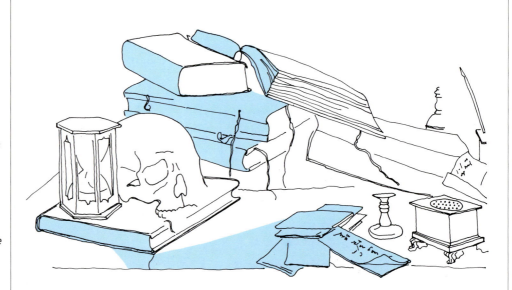

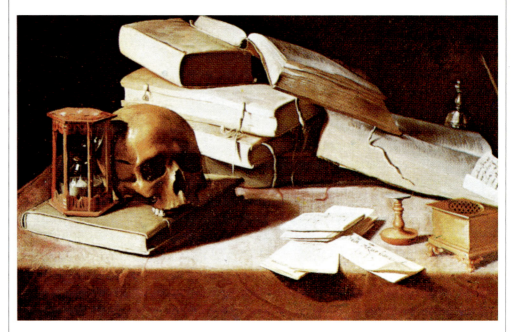

tradition, of realistic painting as early as the 15th century.

Of the other traditional genres of northern European painting, one must at least be mentioned, the large scenes of biblical or plebeian subjects, forming a vast representation, whether peasant or aristocratic, of an entire human universe.

This type of painting reached its highest point at a time preceding almost all the painters mentioned here, in the work of followers of the great Brueghel, among them his son Pieter the Younger. It is nevertheless appropriate to include it in any account of Baroque painting, for the grandiose atmosphere in these paintings was based on the juxtaposition of strong colors, energetic movement, dramatic contrast, and above all on unbridled, prodigious, exultant, and almost demonic fantasy: in short, all that was most Baroque.

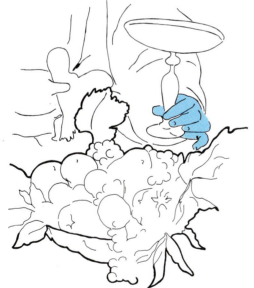

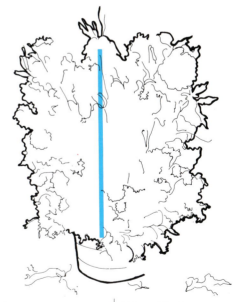

Above left
Caravaggio, still life detail from Bacchus; Florence, Uffizi.
Caravaggio, who started Baroque painting by studying the contrasts of light, is also representative in a different sense. He was a highly skilled painter of still lifes, an inclination that also emerges in pictures apparently dedicated to other subjects, but in which the artist's true interest is the portrayal of everyday life.

Above right
Jan Breughel, Flower Vase; Munich, Alte Pinakothek.
The most traditional subject of still life is the vase of flowers. The Flemish painters of the late 16th century were the main initiators of this genre, and this subject was common in all countries affected by the Baroque style. As in this case, the Flemish taste is visible in the way the brightly colored flowers stand out from the dark background.

273

Pieter Breughel the Elder,
The Tower of Babel, *detail,
Vienna, Kunsthistorisches
Museum.*
The great tower seems to
bear down on the scene
played out at its base, but
balance is restored by color
references that link the
focal points of the work.

The "infernal" landscape
Another success of the
Baroque period was the
"infernal" landscape, which
provided a scope for its love
of drama and the grandiose.
The love of light effects led
to the organization of the
painting around ones that
highlight important areas.

SCULPTURE

*Francesco Duquesnoy,
Sacred Love Brings Down
Profane Love; Rome,
Galleria Spada.
A sfumato suggesting
mellowness and indefinite
transparency achieves a
pictorial effect on this
marble with its fine reliefs
depicting putti at play. This
artist specialized in such
effects and was much
appreciated by collectors of
the time.*

The Baroque period did not lack sculptors, although few of them were outstanding – perhaps only Gian Lorenzo Bernini, who was even greater as a sculptor than as an architect. Sculpture was perhaps the most characteristic art form of the Baroque age and was certainly the most widespread. Not only did it succeed, unlike architecture and painting, in the creation of an artistic idiom largely common to all Europe, but it affected almost every artistic artifact produced during that period. In short, the first recognizable characteristic of Baroque sculpture is its omnipresence.
Sculptures produced in this period can be divided into two broad categories: those intended for decoration, to add the finishing touches to architecture; and sculpture in the usual sense of the word, a work in itself. Architecture made use of decorative sculpture in three distinct ways. The first was in the form of a horizontal line of statues

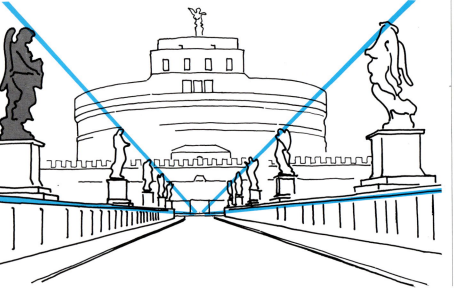

***Architectural function in
sculpture***
*The first concern of Baroque
sculptors was to blend their
work with that of the other
arts. Here it is impossible to
separate the two: the whole
is clearly architectural, but
the main part is played by
the statues on the sides of
the bridge, which draw the
perspective toward Castel
Sant'Angelo.*

or other sculptures to complete the top of a building. Again this was not a Baroque invention, but in the Baroque period it became a conventional stylistic feature. It derived from the custom, fashionable in the 17th century, of crowning a building with an "attic." In effect this was a low parapet concealing the sloping roof and gave the building, seen from below, the appearance of ending in a horizontal line. This feature came to be almost always decorated with a row of statues regularly placed and standing out against the sky. The distance between one statue and another was equal to that between one column or pilaster and another on the façade of a building (in architectural terms, the intercolumniation). Examples include St. Peter's, Rome, the oval colonnade of which was the work of Bernini himself, the palace of Versailles, and dozens of other buildings, large and small. From the attic or roof of a building the practice was extended to other horizontals – the walls enclosing gardens, the parapets of bridges, and so on. Another architectural use of sculptural elements such as statues was to replace columns as supporting features, whether as caryatids (female figures) or telamons (male ones). This use dates back to

Melchiorre Caffà, Ecstasy of St. Catherine of Siena; *Rome, church of Santa Caterina, Magnanapoli. The subject of ecstasy is here treated with exceptional fluidity and lightness; the marble dematerializes in flowing robes and clouds that blend into the veined alabaster background to suggest an unreal spatiality.*

Gian Lorenzo Bernini and assistants, statues on the bridge of Sant'Angelo, Rome. The idea of a row of statues placed at regular intervals to complete an architectural composition already existed but the Baroque made it a distinctive feature. The statues are usually placed on the so-called "attic" of a building. As here, they can even be used to "furnish" an urban complex.

277

classical Greece and was in great vogue in the Baroque produced in Austria and Germany. The third and most typical use of sculpture in combination with architecture was in friezes, groupings of coats-of-arms, scrolls, trophies, and similar elements. Here, sculpture "completed" Baroque buildings; it was sometimes even a "means" to conceal imperfect "joins" such as the unsuccessful combination of two architectural motifs. This even reached the point where the sculpture seems to be, or actually becomes, architecture, as in Bernini's baldacchino in St. Peter's, in which

Left
Pierre Puget, Blessed Virgin; *Genoa, Oratory of San Filippo.*

The motif of the spiral column

This is another work of sculpture that can, with some reason, be considered architecture and presents many of the most typical Baroque features: grandiosity, fantasy, theatricality. One element destined to meet with huge success was the spiral column, a predominant feature of the baldacchino.

Gian Lorenzo Bernini, baldacchino in St. Peter's, Rome.
This was built in proportion to the immense space around it and is truly colossal, as high as a nine-story building. Nevertheless, it has maintained some of the artifices found in the processional baldacchinos it is based on – the great Baroque love of "deception." So for example the large fringes are slightly disturbed as if moved by the breeze, great bees –

taken from the coat of arms of the commissioning pope – "walk" on the columns.

the roles of the two forms mingle to a degree very much in keeping with Baroque taste. Such, then, were the ways in which sculpture was used with architecture. The work traditionally undertaken by the sculptor in former ages, on tombs, altars, commemorative monuments and the like, still continued to be produced in the Baroque period. Designs generally approached, or could even be taken for, scenography, with a theatrical effect – perhaps appropriate in a period that saw the rise of melodrama and the modern theater. In a side-chapel Bernini presents the ecstasy of a saint as a theatrical event, with members of the family who commissioned the work portrayed life-size, seated in boxes just as though at the theater. The sculpture used in these works had two outstanding characteristics. First, it was technically perfect. Such was the mastery of the sculptors over their material that in statues carved from marble it is impossible to deduce or imagine the original shape of the block. Michelangelo, summarizing the ideals of the Renaissance, said that a statue should look as if it could roll down from the top of a hill to the bottom without being harmed. No such

thing could be said of Baroque sculptures. They have what might be called a photographic objective – to fix a movement. This involves the use of free, loose design, and also human forms far more slender than those considered desirable by Renaissance artists.

In sculpture the other particular characteristic of the period – and the most important – was the representation of movement. Figures are never depicted immobile or in attitudes of repose but always in motion, and most typically at that moment of least equilibrium which is the climax of a movement, the imperceptible but dramatic moment, for example, when a vaulter is no longer rising but has not yet begun to descend and is motionless, in an attitude of potential, in mid-air. This preference for movement explains the success of the *figura serpentinata,* the serpentine figure, in the 17th century. This way of representing the human figure first came to the fore in the second half of the 16th century, the period immediately preceding the Baroque. The figure was depicted in the act of performing a spiral movement, the result of swift rotation like that of an athlete throwing the discus. Robes are full, billowing in the wind, ideal for the

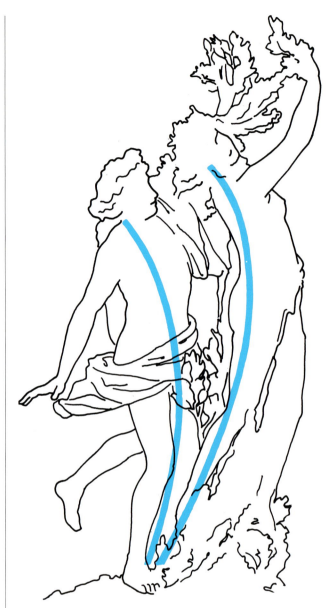

dramatic contrasts of light and shade so typical of the period. Sometimes the composition became exaggerated in a way suggestive more of agitation than of motion. The artist was sometimes so enamored with the effects he was producing with his technical skill that he lost sight of the overall harmony. This can always happen, however, when the work of masters is passed on to be repeated by workers. One merit of the Baroque was that it created conditions in which second-rate work could be assimilated into the execution of complex works of greater artistic value: the great fountains inhabited by bearded figures, satyrs, nymphs, dolphins, and assorted monsters that adorned the piazzas and the avenues of Baroque cities and gardens, the decoration of the great staircases in the palaces of the time, down to the stucco work and other profuse ornamentation of galleries, salons, churches – in every sort of interior. Sometimes, the general impression created was merely orgiastic; usually Baroque style achieved an effect of triumph.

Above
Unstable equilibrium
G. L. Bernini, *Apollo and Daphne; Rome, Galleria Borghese. The curves of the bodies come together, suggesting the moment when the nymph is turned into a laurel tree to escape the pursuing god.*

Right
G. L. Bernini, *Monument of the Blessed Ludovica Albertoni; Rome, San Francesco a Ripa.*

Glossary

ABBEY In the strict sense, a monastery run by an abbot. Widespread in the Romanesque period, its characteristic architectural features include a church with a larger apse than usual, to accomodate the numerous officiating monks; a large hall (called a chapter house) for the monks' meetings, and one or more cloisters.

ALTARPIECE A painting or, less often, a sculpture in low relief, placed over the altar. It sometimes consists of several panels when it is called a polyptych; paintings on two panels are known as diptychs, those on three, triptychs.

AMBULATORY A continuation of the aisles around the choir (see chevet).

APSE A semicircular or polygonal projection at the east end of the church, behind the main altar. Semicircular, square or polygonal in form, some churches have three, five or more apses. In these cases the central apse is nearly always larger than the others. Some churches have the apse along the two short sides, a characteristic feature of German Romanesque. Sometimes as well as that at the east end of the church, there are apses on the end walls of the transepts. If the east end and transept apses are the same size it is called a triconch apse.

ARCH A curved architectural structure created using stone or brick voussoirs. The arch may be in a wall or supported by columns or piers. The main characteristic is that it transmits its own weight and that of the structure supported in a downward curve and therefore tends to push its supports outward; this must be countered in some way – by adding another arch, creating thrust in the opposite direction (buttress), or connecting the lowest courses of the arch with an iron chain. The arch can be round, pointed (typical of Gothic), segmental or elliptical – the latter two much used in Baroque art.

The parts of the arch are the intrados, or internal curve, and the extrados, external curve, a span and the rise or height.

ARCADING Characteristic in Romanesque architecture (especially in Italy and Germany), this is a row of small arches set at the top of a wall, beneath the eaves or moulding, and occasionally used to mark a string-course.

ARCHITRAVE The horizontal element connecting two columns or piers. In the architectural orders this is the lowest part of the entablature. Its decoration varies according to the order.

ATTIC An architectural structure placed around a roof to conceal it from below. Sometimes the word is used to denote the top story of a building.

BALDACCHINO A projecting architectural element above Gothic statues placed in niches on the outside of churches, or a canopy, usually supported by columns, above an altar.

BALUSTRADE A typical Baroque parapet made of small shaped columns or pillars, called balusters, that support a rail or coping.

BARREL VAULT A semicylindrical vault.

BASE The lower part of a column or pier. Also used for the lower part of a building, usually treated differently from the rest.

BAY The space enclosed by a vault and the columns or piers sustaining it. The term is often used to denote the space between two supports linked by an arch.

BUTTRESS A masonry structure on the outside wall of a building designed to reinforce it and transmit the thrust of a vault or arch to the ground.

CHIAROSCURO In painting, the use of contrasts of light and shade.

CANOPY See Baldacchino

CAPITAL The upper part of a column or pilaster

strip. Usually this is the most characteristic part of the column, and is used to distinguish one order from another. The Renaissance had five types: Doric, Tuscan, Ionic, Corinthian and Composite. The first two had an abacus at the top, in the form of a slab, the third had characteristic volutes, spiral scrolls on each corner. The last two feature acanthus leaves (a Mediterranean plant).

CARTOON A large sheet of paper on which the painter draws the picture before transferring it to canvas or, in the case of a fresco, to the plaster.

COLUMN An architectural support, usually cylindrical and freestanding. This is the most characteristic feature of an architectural order. The classical ones have a base, shaft, capital and different names according to the design: fluted if the shaft has vertical grooves, cabled if the grooves are then filled for a third of the way up; spiral if the shaft is grooved in twisting lines. This latter type is very common in Baroque architecture.

CHEVET The characteristic termination of French (and other) medieval churches featuring a number of radiating chapels set around the corridor (ambulatory) of the central apse.

CHOIR The part of the church where the choir singers sit, usually situated behind the main altar. In conventual churches it is used only by monks and in Romanesque examples is often particularly complex in form. The term is also used to describe the entire eastern arm of a church.

CLERESTORY In Romanesque and Gothic churches the upper stage of the main walls above the aisles that is pierced by windows.

CLOISTER Characteristic of monastic architecture, this is a covered passage around an open space connecting the church with the other parts of the complex (chapter-house, refectory, monks' cells).

CRYPT Literally the "hidden part" of a church. In Romanesque and later churches the small cell or church beneath the main altar where the relics of a saint are kept.

CYMATIUM The top member of a cornice in a classical entablature. It later came to be the top of a painted panel, door or window or any decorative termination to a building.

COMPOSITE One of the architectural orders elaborated by the Romans and used again during the Renaissance and Baroque periods. Particularly rich in decoration, it combined the Corinthian and Ionic orders.

CORBEL Any long narrow architectural feature that projects from a wall. It is now used for a projection supporting beams or cornices.

CORINTHIAN One of the three Greek architectural orders, used widely by the Romans and during the Renaissance and Baroque periods. It is mainly distinguished by the acanthus-leaf decoration of its capitals.

CORNICE The projecting ornamental moulding around the top of a building usually sustained by a corbel. Most are shaped and divided into characteristic bands.

CROSS or GROIN VAULT This is produced by crossing two barrel vaults; if the arches at the base of the vault and the ribs are pointed, the cross will tend upwards and is known as a rib vault.

DIPTYCH A religious painting on two equal panels generally used to decorate small altars.

DOME An architectural structure used to cover a building; ideally this has an even curve and is erected on a circular base. It can be made up of several cells each starting from one side of a polygon (usually an octagon). There is generally a small round templet at the top – the lantern – which allows light in. The most common dome has a circular base, but the Baroque period developed many more complex ones.

DORIC A Greek architectural order later used with some modifications by Renaissance, Baroque and later architects. It features a simple capital consisting of an echinus and abacus and the frieze, or central part of the architrave, between the two columns, decorated with metope and triglyphs: decorative (usually sculpted) and fluted panels.

DRUM The cylindrical or polygonal architectural structure supporting a dome and discharging its weight onto the arches beneath it.

EMBRASURE A recess for a window or door, usually splayed on the inside. It emphasizes the entrance and allows more light to enter; Gothic artists applied rich sculptural decorations to this, especially around doors.

ENTABLATURE The upper part of a given order consisting of architrave, frieze, and cornice.

FAÇADE The external covering on the front of a building. By extension, the term is sometimes used for the treatment applied to the façade.

FACING The finish on the surface of a wall.

FRONTAL The front part of an altar artistically decorated.

FLYING BUTTRESS A structure in the form of a half-arch, raised on the exterior of a building to cancel the thrust of the vaults through the ribs by discharging it onto the buttresses.

FORESHORTENING The representation of a figure placed not horizontally or vertically in relation to the viewer but obliquely, so that some parts appear near and others farther away. The reason for the term is that such bodies (or objects) appear shorter than in reality.

FRESCO A technique of wall painting that consists of applying paint to a very thin layer of plaster while it is still fresh. The color penetrates the plaster becoming an integral part of the wall itself and is thus indelible.

GREEK CROSS The type of plan found in churches made up of four equal arms.

GARDEN Three types of garden complete a building, "Italian," with geometrical flower beds and hedges, arranged around statues and fountains, not very large, and typically architectural in structure; "French" which came into fashion in the baroque period, with large ponds and lawns, imposing in size and with tree-lined avenues disappearing into the distance; "English," which tends to imitate the spontaneous growth of nature.

GARGOYLE The terminal part of a spout which projects from the building to discharge rainwater at a distance from the wall.

GROTESQUE Painting decoration typical of the late Renaissance and Baroque periods. It consists mainly of vegetable and fanciful motifs animated and intertwined. The name is apparently derived from frescoes found in the thermal baths of Titus in Rome, in the Renaissance considered practically natural grottoes.

HALL CHURCH or HALLENKIRCHE A type of church peculiar to German-speaking areas with aisles all the same height.

ILLUMINATION Painting on parchment or paper, executed in small dimensions.

IONIC A much-used architectural order distinguished mainly by its scrolled capitals.

KEYSTONE The central stone of an arch or rib vault, sometimes decorated.

LADY CHAPEL Typical of English churches, this is dedicated to the Virgin Mary and usually situated at the east end of the church, behind the choir.

LANTERN A polygonal architectural structure enclosing and masking the central dome of a church. Its weight helps to counter the external thrust of the dome.

LATIN CROSS The type of plan found in churches in which the longitudinal body, consisting of one or more aisles, is much longer than the two side arms of the transept.

LESENE A half pilaster sunk in the wall of a building for decorative purposes. It resembles a column in form and is sometimes decorated.

LOGGIA An arcade open on one or more sides.

MAJESTY Painting depicting Christ or the Virgin enthroned and surrounded by angels, saints or sometimes figures connected with the story in question.

MANDORLA An almond-shaped outline containing a holy figure, always placed at the center of a composition.

MOSAIC A surface decorated with small pieces of stone or colored ceramics fitted together to produce the picture desired. This can be applied to floor or walls. A typical Byzantine skill, transmitted to many Romanesque works, is mosaic with figures standing out against a uniform gold tesserae background.

MULLIONED WINDOW A window divided by vertical uprights to create two or more lights.

MULTIFOILED A structure with several foils, semicircular lobe-shaped projections or curves.

NAVE The western limb of a church. The term is also often applied only to the central nave between two rows of arches or columns.

NICHE A wall recess usually semicylindrical and vertical in form used for decorative purposes. The niches of Gothic churches house the statues that adorn the exterior.

OIL PAINTING A form of painting in which the medium used to bind the pigments or colors is a vegetable oil (usually linseed or walnut oil).

ORIENTATION In western churches the main axis generally lies west-east. The main entrance is at the west end, the altar at the east end.

PIER A support in various forms, usually sturdier than a column; it is quadrangular, polygonal or multifoiled in section. The cross-shaped pier was typical of Romanesque, one half-column set against another. The compound pier is also common and consists of sometimes eight or even more shafts.

PINNACLE A slender conical or pyramidal spire crowning a buttress. Not only a decoration, it also adds weight to the buttress and thus enables it better to absorb the thrust of the flying buttresses.

POLYPTYCH An altarpiece made up of several pieces or panels, joined together. Sometimes it has hinges and can be folded.

PORCH An atrium doorway or aedicola that is typical of Romanesque architecture. This has a vault supporting a sloping roof, or a second smaller aedicola (tribune) resting on two columns, often sustained by statues of crouching lions. The term can also apply more generally to a vestibule.

PORTAL The main monumental doorway into a church, usually richly decorated.

RIB A part of the vault that highlights the points of greatest static tension and connects the supports of the vault (columns, piers, etc.) to the keystone, creating the webs of the vault.

ROSE WINDOW Large round window divided by tracery on the façade of a church (and sometimes those of the transepts).

RUSTICATION The outside covering of a building featuring blocks of stone that project from the wall. Cut in various forms, when called diamond-point, all the stones are cut in the form of a pyramid.

SCROLL A typical Baroque decoration used in painting and sculpture (and often applied as an architectural decoration). Originally it always had an inscription, but was later used for ornament alone.

SERLIANA A type of window with three openings, the central one arched and the side ones with architraves. Already known in Roman times it was advocated in the Renaissance by the writer and architect Serlio.

SFUMATO A method of painting using indistinct outlines.

SPIRE A pointed conical or pyramidal architectural structure used to crown and decorate towers, bell towers and the upper parts of Gothic cathedrals in general. It consists of a base and an elongated pyramid.

SPLAYING A characteristic way of cutting walls obliquely to obtain a large opening on one side and a narrower passage on the other side. It may be single or double, repeated twice in the wall with reversed inclination.

SPOLVERO A fresco technique by which the cartoon is transferred to the plaster by passing charcoal powder through a number of small holes made on the lines drawn on the cartoon.

STIACCIATO A term describing a technique for making reliefs with a minimum of projection.

STUCCO A material used for decoration or modeling; it dries very slowly and is easily worked. Mainly used on interiors, it was highly popular in the Baroque and subsequent Rococo periods.

TEMPERA A painting technique based on the use of colors diluted in water and mixed with a binding substance (originally fish glue, egg yolk, fig tree sap etc.) to make the color adhere to the support (wood, paper, canvas etc.).

TRANSEPT The transverse part of a church intersects with the nave to produce the characteristic cross plan.

TRIBUNE A gallery (usually covered with a vault) situated above the aisles and overlooking the nave.

TRIFORIUM A small arched gallery usually with three-lights above the aisles of a church overlooking the nave.

TRUMEAU A pillar, or stone element, dividing an opening or doorway and supporting the lintel.

TRUSS A triangular timber structure used to bridge a space and be self-supporting.

TYMPANUM The area between the lintel of a doorway and the arch above it.

VAULT An arched roof or ceiling resting on four supports. The barrel, or tunnel, vault is semicylindrical; the groin vault is created by the intersection at right angles of two barrel vaults. The rib vault is pointed and sustained by ribs and has cells.

VOUSSOIR A wedge-shaped arch stone.

WEBB or CELL This is the term given to each of the four triangular sections created in the cross vault.

FURTHER READING

Compiled by Geraldine White

ROMANESQUE ART

GENERAL

Atroshenko, V.I., *The Origins of the Romanesque: Near Eastern Influences on European Art, 4th-12th Centuries*, Woodstock, New York: Overlook Press, 1986; London: Lund Humphries, 1985

Beckwith, John, *Early Medieval Art: Carolingian, Ottonian, Romanesque*, New York: Praeger, and London: Thames and Hudson, 1964

Collon-Gevaert, Suzanne, Jean Lejeune and Jacques Stiennon, *A Treasury of Romanesque Art: Metalwork, Illuminations and Sculpture from the Valley of the Meuse*, New York and London: Phaidon, 1972 (French original, 1961)

Dodwell, Charles Reginald, *The Pictorial Arts of the West, 800-1200*, New Haven, Connecticut, and London: Yale University Press, 1993

Evans, Joan, *Cluniac Art of the Romanesque Period*, Cambridge: Cambridge University Press, 1950

Focillon, Henri, *The Art of the West in the Middle Ages. Vol. 1, Romanesque Art*, New York and London: Phaidon, 1963; 3rd edition, Oxford: Phaidon, 1980 (French original, 1938)

Green, Rosalie, *Studies in Ottonian, Romanesque, and Gothic Art*, London: Pindar Press, 1994

Kuhnel, Bianca, *Crusader Art of the Twelfth Century: A Geographical, an Historical, or an Art Historical Notion?* Berlin: Mann, 1994

Nichols, Stephen G., *Romanesque Signs: Early Medieval Narrative and Iconography*, New Haven, Connecticut: Yale University

Press, 1983

Petzold, Andreas, *Romanesque Art*, New York: Abrams, and London: Weidenfeld and Nicolson, 1995

Swarzenski, Hanns, *Monuments of Romanesque Art: The Art of Church Treasures in North-Western Europe*, Chicago: University of Chicago Press, 1954; 2nd edition, 1967, and London: Faber

Timmers, J.J.M., *A Handbook of Romanesque Art*, New York: Macmillan, and London: Nelson, 1969 (Dutch original, 1965)

Toman, Rolf (editor), *Die Kunst der Romanik: Architektur, Skulptur, Malerei*, Cologne: Könemann, 1996

Zarnecki, George, *Romanesque Art*, New York: Universe, and London: Weidenfeld and Nicolson, 1971; as *Romanesque*, New York: Universe, and London: Herbert, 1989

Britain

Macready, Sarah and Frederick Hugh Thompson (editors), *Art and Patronage in the English Romanesque*, London: Society of Antiquaries, 1986

Zarnecki, George, Janet Holt and Tristram Holland (editors), *English Romanesque Art, 1066-1200: Hayward Gallery, London, 5 April-8 July 1984*, London: Weidenfeld and Nicolson in association with the Arts Council of Great Britain, 1984

France

Aubert, Marcel, *L'art Roman en France*, Paris: Flammarion, 1961

Mâle, Émile, *Religious Art in France, the Twelfth Century: A Study of the Origins of Medieval Iconography*, Princeton, New Jersey: Princeton University Press, 1977 (French original, 1910)

Germany

Legner, Anton, *Deutsche Kunst der Romanik*, Munich: Hirmer, 1982; as *Romanische Kunst in Deutschland*, 1996

Italy

Decker, Heinrich, *Romanesque Art in Italy*, New York: Abrams, 1959 (German original, 1958); London: Thames and Hudson, 1958

Spain

Bango Torviso, Isidro Gonzalo, *El románico en España*, Madrid: Espasa Calpe, 1992

Camps Cazorla, Emilio, *El arte románico en España*, Barcelona: Labor, 1935

Gómez-Moreno, Manuel, *El arte románico español*, Madrid: Blass, 1934

Palol, Pedro de and Max Hirmer, *Early Medieval Art in Spain*, New York: Abrams, and London: Thames and Hudson, 1967 (German original, 1965)

ARCHITECTURE

Allsopp, Bruce, *Romanesque Architecture: the Romanesque Achievement*, New York: Day, and London: Barker, 1971

Busch, Harald, *Romanesque Europe*, New York: Macmillan, 1960; London: Batsford, 1959 (German original, 1959)

Clapham, Alfred William, *Romanesque Architecture in Western Europe*, Oxford: Clarendon Press, 1936

Conant, Kenneth John, *Carolingian and Romanesque Architecture, 800-1200*, Baltimore and Harmondsworth: Penguin, 1959; 2nd integrated edition, reprinted with corrections, 1987

Dehio, Georg, *Die Kirchliche Baukunst des Abendlandes. Bd. 1, Der christlich-antike Stil, der romanische Stil*, Stuttgart: Cotta, 1892-1901

Fernie, Eric, *Romanesque Architecture: Design, Meaning and Metrology*, London: Pindar Press, 1995

Héliot, Pierre M.L., *Du carolingien au gothique: l'évolution de la plastique murale dans l'architecture religieuse du Nord-Ouest de l'Europe (IXe-XIIIe siècles)*, Paris: Imprimerie nationale, 1966

Krautheimer, Rudolf, "An Introduction to an 'Iconography of Medieval Architecture,'" *Journal of the Warburg and Courtauld Institutes*, 5 (1942): 1[-]33

Kubach, Hans Erich, *Romanesque Architecture*, New York: Abrams, 1975 (Italian original, 1972)

Kubach, Hans Erich, *Romanische Hallenkirchen in Europa*, Mainz: von Zabern, 1997

Puig y Cadafalch, José, *La geografia i els orígens del primer Art romànic*, Barcelona, 1930

Radding, Charles, *Medieval Architecture, Medieval Learning: Builders and Masters in the Age of Romanesque and Gothic*, New Haven, Connecticut, and London: Yale University Press, 1992

Saalman, Howard, *Medieval Architecture: European Architecture, 600-1200*, New York: Braziller, and London: Prentice-Hall, 1962

Stewart, Cecil, *Early Christian, Byzantine and Romanesque Architecture*, New York and London: Longmans Green, 1954

Stratford, Neil (editor), *Romanesque and Gothic: Essays for George Zarnecki*, Woodbridge, Suffolk: Boydell Press, 1987

Britain
Clapham, Alfred William, *English Romanesque Architecture Before the Conquest*, Oxford: Clarendon Press, 1930

Clapham, Alfred William, *English Romanesque Architecture After the Conquest*, Oxford: Clarendon Press, 1934

Clapham, Alfred William, *Romanesque Architecture in England*, New York and London: for the British Council by Longmans Green, 1950

France
Anfray, Marcel, *L'architecture normande: son influence dans le nord de France aux XIe et XIIe siècles*, Paris: Picard,1939

Evans, Joan, *Romanesque Architecture of the Order of Cluny*, Cambridge: Cambridge University Press, 1938

Hubert, Jean, *L'architecture religieuse de haut Moyen Âge en France: plans, notices et bibliographie*, Paris: Imprimerie nationale, 1952

Lasteyrie, Robert de, *L'architecture religieuse en France à l'époque romane*, Paris: Picard, 1912; 2nd edition, 1929

Italy
Ricci, Corrado, *Romanesque Architecture in Italy*, New York: Heinemann, and London: Brentano, 1925

Salmi, Mario, *L'architettura romanica in Toscana*, Milan: Bestetti & Tuminelli, 1925

Spain
Dodds, Jerrilynn Denise, *Architecture and Ideology in Early Medieval Spain*, University Park: Pennsylvania State University Press, 1990

Whitehill, Walter Muir, *Spanish Romanesque Architecture of the Eleventh Century*, London: Oxford University Press, 1941

SCULPTUREE
Busch, Harald and Bernd Lohse (editors), *Romanesque Sculpture*, London: Batsford, 1962

Focillon, Henri, *L'art des sculpteurs romans: recherches sur l'histoire des formes,* Paris: Leroux,1931

Goldschmidt, Adolf, *Die Elfenbeinskulpturen. Bd. 3-4, Aus der romanischen Zeit XI.-XIII. Jahrhundert*, Berlin: Cassirer, 1923-26

Hearn, Millard Fillmore, *Romanesque Sculpture: The Revival of Monumental Stone Sculpture in the Eleventh and Twelfth Centuries*, Ithaca, New York: Cornell University Press, and Oxford: Phaidon, 1981

Kahn, Deborah (editor), *The Romanesque Frieze and Its Spectator: The Lincoln Symposium Papers*, New York, Miller, and London: Oxford University Press, 1992

Liévaux-Boccador, Jacqueline and Édouard Bresset, *Statuaire médiévale de collection*, Zug: Clefs du temps, 1972

Panofsky, Erwin, *Tomb Sculpture: Four Lectures on Its Changing Aspects from Ancient Egypt to Bernini*, New York and London: Abrams, 1964

Porter, Arthur Kingsley, *Romanesque Sculpture of the Pilgrimage Roads*, Boston: Marshall Jones, 1923

Williamson, Paul, *Catalogue of Romanesque Sculpture*, London: Victoria and Albert Museum, 1983

Young, Brian, *The Villein's Bible: Stories in Romanesque Carving*, London: Barrie and Jenkins, 1990

Zarnecki, George, *Studies in Romanesque Sculpture*, London: Dorian Press, 1979

Zarnecki, George, *Further Studies in Romanesque Sculpture*, London: Pindar Press, 1992

Britain
Heyward, Ben (editor), *Romanesque Stone Sculpture from Medieval England*, Leeds: Henry Moore Sculpture Trust, 1993

Saxl, Frits, *English Sculptures of the Twelfth Century*, Boston: Boston Book and Art Shop, and London: Faber, 1954

Stone, Lawrence, *Sculpture in Britain: The Middle Ages*, Baltimore and Harmondsworth,: Penguin, 1955; 2nd edition, 1972

Zarnecki, George, *English Romanesque Sculpture, 1066-1140*, London: Tiranti, 1951

Zarnecki, George, *Later English Romanesque Sculpture,1140-1210*, London: Tiranti, 1953

France
Armi, C. Edson, *Masons and Sculptors in Romanesque Burgundy: The New Aesthetic of Cluny III*, University Park and London: Pennsylvania State University Press, 1983

Deschamps, Paul, *French Sculpture of the Romanesque Period, Eleventh and Twelfth Centuries*, New York: Harcourt Brace, and Florence: Pantheon, 1930

Forsyth, Ilene H., *The Throne of Wisdom: Wood Sculptures of the Madonna in Romanesque France*, Princeton, New Jersey: Princeton University Press, 1972

Schapiro, Meyer, *The Sculpture of Moissac*, London: Thames and Hudson, 1985

Germany
Beenken, Hermann, *Romanische Skulptur in Deutschland (11. und 12. Jahrhundert)*, Leipzig: Klinkhardt & Biermann, 1924

Italy
Crichton, George Henderson, *Romanesque Sculpture in Italy*, London: Routledge, 1954

Spain
Gaillard, Georges, *Les débuts de la sculpture romane espagnol: Leon, Jaca, Compostelle*, Paris: Hartmann, 1938

Porter, Arthur Kingsley, *Spanish Romanesque Sculpture,* Florence: Pantheon, and Paris: Pegasus, 1928

Trens, Manuel, *Les majestats catalanes*, Barcelona: Alpha, 1967

PAINTING
Ainaud de Lasarte, Juan and André Held, *Romanesque Painting,* London: Weidenfeld and Nicolson, 1963

Anthony, Edgar Waterman, *Romanesque Frescoes*, Princeton, New Jersey: Princeton University Press, 1951

Boeckler, Albert, *Abendländische Miniaturen bis zum Ausgang der romanischen Zeit*, Berlin and Leipzig: de Gruyter, 1930

Cahn, Walter, *Romanesque Manuscripts: the Twelfth Century*, London: Miller, 1996

Caviness, Madeline Harrison, *Paintings on Glass: Studies in Romanesque and Gothic Monumental Art*, Aldershot and Brookfield, Vermont: Variorum, 1997

Demus, Otto, *Romanesque Mural Painting*, New York: Abrams, and London: Thames and Hudson, 1970 (German original, 1968)

Grabar, André and Carl Nordenfalk, *Romanesque Painting from the Eleventh to the Thirteenth Century*, New York: Skira, 1938

Kauffmann, Claus Michael, *Romanesque Manuscripts, 1066-1190*, Boston: New York Graphic Society, and London: Miller, 1975

Swarzenski, Hanns, *Early Medieval Illumination*, New York and Oxford: Oxford University Press, 1951

Turner, D.H., *Romanesque Illuminated Manuscripts in the British Museum*, London: British Museum, 1966

Wettstein, Janine, *La fresque romane*, Paris: Arts et métiers graphiques, and Geneva: Droz, 1971-78

Britain

Cather, Sharon, David Park and Paul Williamson (editors), *Early Medieval Wall Painting and Painted Sculpture in England*, Oxford: B.A.R., 1990

Rickert, Margaret Josephine, *Painting in Britain: The Middle Ages*, Baltimore and London: Penguin, 1954; 2nd edition, 1965

France

Deschamps, Paul, *La peinture murale en France: le haut Moyen Âge et l'époque romane*, Paris: Plon, 1951

Kupfer, Marcia A., *Romanesque Wall Painting in Central France: The Politics of Narrative*, New Haven, Connecticut, and London: Yale University Press, 1993

Italy

Bologna, Ferdinando, *Early Italian Painting: Romanesque and Early Medieval Art*, Princeton, New Jersey: Van Nostrand, 1963

Garrison, Edward B., *Italian Romanesque Panel Painting: an Illustrated Index*, Florence: Olschki, 1949; new edition on CD-ROM, London: Courtauld Institute of Art, 1998

Spain

Sureda, Joan, *La pintura románica en España*, Madrid: Alianza, 1985

APPLIED ARTS

Bloch, Peter, *Romanische Bronzekruzifixe*, Berlin: Deutscher Verlag für Kunstwissenschaft, 1992

Brisac, Catherine, *A Thousand Years of Stained Glass*, New York: Doubleday, and London: Macdonald, 1986 (French original, 1985)

Campbell, Marian, *An Introduction to Medieval Enamels*, London: HMSO, and Owings Mills, Maryland: Stemmer House, 1983

Cowen, Painton, *Rose Windows*, San Francisco: Chronicle, and London: Thames and Hudson, 1979

Grodecki, Louis, *Le vitrail roman*, Fribourg: Office du livre, 1977

Lasko, Peter, *Ars sacra, 800-1200*, Baltimore and Harmondsworth: Penguin, 1972; 2nd edition, New Haven, Connecticut, and London: Yale University Press, 1994

Perry, John Tavenor, *Dinanderie: A History and Description of Medieval Art Work in Copper, Brass and Bronze*. New York: Macmillan, and London: Allen, 1910

St. Clair, Archer and Elizabeth Parker McLachan (editors), *The Carver's Art: Medieval Sculpture in Ivory, Bone and Horn*, New Brunswick, New Jersey: Jane Voorhees Zimmerli Art Museum, 1989

Stratford, Neil, *Catalogue of the Medieval Enamels in the British Museum. Vol. 2, Northern Romanesque Enamels*, London: British Museum Press, 1993

GOTHIC ART

GENERAL

Aubert, Marcel, *High Gothic Art*, London: Methuen, 1964

Bialostocki, Jan, *Spätmittelalter und beginnende Neuzeit*, Berlin: Propyläen, 1972

Brown, Reginald Allen, Howard Montagu Colvin and Arnold Joseph Taylor, *The History of the King's Works. Vols. 1-2*, London: HMSO, 1963

Camille, Michael, *The Gothic Idol: Ideology and Image-Making in Medieval Art*, New York and Cambridge: Cambridge University Press, 1989

Camille, Michael, *Gothic Art: Glorious Visions*, New York: Abrams, and London: Weidenfeld and Nicolson, 1996

DuColombier, Pierre, *Les Chantiers des Cathédrals: Ouvriers, Architectes, Sculpteurs*, Paris: Picard, 1953; new edition, 1973

Focillon, Henri, *The Art of the West in the Middle Ages. Vol. 2, Gothic Art*, New York and London: Phaidon, 1963; 3rd edition, 1980

Frankl, Paul Theodore, *The Gothic: Literary Sources and Interpretation Through Eight Centuries*, Princeton, New Jersey: Princeton University Press, 1960

Frisch, Teresa Grace, *Gothic Art, 1140-1450: Sources and Documents*, Englewood Cliffs, New Jersey: Prentice-Hall, 1971

Green, Rosalie, *Studies in Ottonian, Romanesque, and Gothic Art*, London: Pindar Press, 1994

Harvey, John Hooper, *The Gothic World, 1100-1600: A Survey of Architecture and Art*, New York and London: Batsford, 1950

Huizinga, Johan, *The Waning of the Middle Ages: A Study of the Forms of Life, Thought, and Art in France and the Netherlands in the XIVth and and XVth Centuries*, London: Arnold, and Garden City, New York: Doubleday, 1924; as *The autumn of the Middle Ages*, Chicago: University of Chicago Press, 1996 (Dutch original, 1919)

Huth, Hans, *Künstler und Werkstatt der Spätgotik*, Augsburg: Filser, 1923; 4th edition, Darmstadt: Wissen-schaftliche Buchgesellschaft, 1981

Martindale, Andrew, *Gothic Art*, New York: Oxford University Press, and London: Thames and Hudson, 1967

Martindale, Andrew, *The Rise of the Artist in the Middle Ages and Early Renaissance*, New York: McGraw-Hill, and London: Thames and Hudson, 1972

Simson, Otto Georg von, *Das Mittelalter II: das Hohe Mittelalter*, Berlin: Propyläen, 1972

Stratford, Neil (editor), *Romanesque and Gothic: Essays for George Zarnecki*, Woodbridge, Suffolk: Boydell Press, 1987

Swaan, Wim, *The Late Middle Ages: Art and Architecture from 1350 to the Advent of the Renaissance*, Ithaca, New York: Cornell University Press, and London: Elek, 1977

Britain

Alexander, John and Paul Binski (editors), *Age of Chivalry: Art in Plantagenet England, 1200-1400*, London: Royal Academy of Arts in association with Weidenfeld and Nicolson, 1987

Brieger, Peter H., *English Art, 1216-1307*, Oxford: Clarendon Press, 1957

Germany

Möbius, Friedrich and Helga Sciurie (editors), *Geschichte der deutschen Kunst, 1200-1350*, Leipzig: Seemann, 1989

ARCHITECTURE

Anderson, William, *The Rise of the Gothic*, Salem, New Hampshire: Salem House, and London: Hutchinson, 1985

Branner, *Gothic Architecture*, New York: Braziller, and London: Prentice-Hall, 1961

Dehio, Georg, *Die kirchliche baukunst des Abendlandes, Bd. 2, Der gotische Stil*, Stuttgart: Cotta, 1887-1901

Europäische Kunst um 1400: achte Ausstellung unter den Auspizien des Europarates, Vienna: Kunsthistorisches Museum, 1962

Fitchen, John, *The Construction of Gothic Cathedrals: A Study of Medieval Vault erection*, Oxford: Clarendon Press, 1961

Frankl, Paul Theodore, *Gothic Architecture*, Baltimore and Harmondsworth: Penguin, 1962

Grodecki, Louis, *Gothic Architecture*, New York: Abrams, 1977 (French original, 1976)

Mark, Robert, *Experiments in Gothic Structure*, Cambridge, Massachusetts: MIT Press, 1982

Panofsky, Erwin, *Gothic Architecture and Scholasticism*, Latrobe, Pennsylvania: Archabbey Press, 1951

Radding, Charles, *Medieval Architecture, Medieval Learning: Builders and Masters in the Age of Romanesque and Gothic*, New Haven, Connecticut, and London: Yale University Press, 1992

Raguin, Virginia Chieffo, *Artistic Integration in Gothic Buildings*, Toronto and London: University of Toronto Press, 1995

Stewart, Cecil, *Gothic Architecture*, New York and London: Longman, 1961

Von Simson, Otto, *The Gothic Cathedral: The Origins of Gothic Architecture and the Medieval Concept of Order*, London: Routledge, 1956

Wilson, Christopher, *The Gothic Cathedral: The Architecture of the Great Church, 1130-1530*, London and New York: Thames and Hudson, 1990

Britain
Bony, Jean, *The English Decorated Style: Gothic Architecture Transformed, 1250-1350*, Ithaca, New York: Cornell University Press, and Oxford: Phaidon, 1979

Coldstream, Nicola, *The Decorated Style: Architecture and Ornament, 1240-1360*, Toronto and Buffalo, New York: University of Toronto Press, and London: British Museum Press, 1994

Fergusson, Peter, *Architecture of Solitude: Cistercian Abbeys in Twelfth-Century England*, Princeton, New Jersey: Princeton University Press, 1984

Harvey, John Hooper, *The Perpendicular Style, 1330-1485*, London: Batsford, 1978

Pevsner, Nikolaus and Priscilla Metcalf, *The Cathedrals of England*, New York and Harmondsworth: Viking, 1985

Platt, Colin, *The Castle in Medieval England and Wales*, New York: Barnes and Noble, and London: Secker and Warburg, 1982

Webb, Geoffrey Fairbank, *Architecture in Britain: The Middle Ages*, Baltimore and Harmondsworth: Penguin, 1956; 2nd edition, 1965

France
Aubert, Marcel, *L'architecture cistercienne en France*, Paris: Éditions d'art et d'histoire, 1943; 2nd édition, 1947

Bony, Jean, *French Gothic Architecture of the 12th and 13th Centuries*, Berkeley: University of California Press, 1983

Crosby, Sumner McKnight, *The Royal Abbey of Saint-Denis: From its Beginnings to the Death of Suger, 475-1151*, New Haven, Connecticut: Yale University Press, 1987

Mussat, André, *Le Style Gothique de l'Ouest de la France, XIIe-XIIIe Siècles*, Paris: Picard, 1963

Germany
Eydoux, Henri Paul, *L'architecture des églises cisterciennes d'Allemagne*, Paris: Presses universitaires de France, 1952

Nussbaum, Norbert, *Deutsche Kirchenbaukunst der Gotik: Entwicklung und Bauformern*, Cologne: DuMont, 1985; 2nd edition, Darmstadt: Wissenschaftliche Buchgesellschaft, 1994

Italy
White, John, *Art and Architecture in Italy, 1250-1400*, Baltimore and Harmondsworth: Penguin, 1966; 3rd edition, New Haven and London: Yale University Press, 1993

Spain
Azcárate, José María de, *Arte gótico en España*, Madrid: Catédra, 1990

Lambert, Élie, *L'Art gotique en Espagne aux XIIe et XIII siècles*, Paris: Laurens, 1931

SCULPTURE
Bauch, Kurt, *Das mittelalterlicher Grabbild: figürliche Grabmäler des 11. bis 15. Jahrhunderts in Europa*, New York and Berlin: de Gruyter, 1976

Busch, Harald, *Gothic Sculpture*, New York: Macmillan, and London: Batsford, 1963

Freeden, Max H. von, *Gothic Sculpture: The Intimate Carvings*, Greenwich, Connecticut: New York Graphic Society, and London: Oldbourne Press, 1962

Jullian, René, *La sculpture gothique*, Paris: Laurens, 1965

Lindley, Phillip, *Gothic to Renaissance: Essays on Sculpture in England*, Stamford: Paul Watkins, 1995

Müller, Theodore, *Sculpture in the Netherlands, Germany, France and Spain, 1400-1500*, Baltimore and Harmondsworth: Penguin, 1966

Vöge, Wilhelm, *Bildhauer des Mittelalters: gesammelte Studien*, Berlin: Mann, 1958; 2nd edition, 1995

Williamson, Paul, *Northern Gothic Sculpture, 1200-1450*, London: Victoria and Albert Museum, 1988

Williamson, Paul, *Gothic Sculpture, 1140-1300*, New Haven, Connecticut and London: Yale University Press, 1995

Britain
Gardner, Arthur, *A Handbook of English Medieval Sculpture*, New York: Macmillan, and Cambridge: Cambridge University Press, 1935; as *English Medieval Sculpture*, Cambridge: Cambridge University Press, 1951

Stone, Lawrence, *Sculpture in Britain: the Middle Ages*, Baltimore and Harmondsworth: Penguin, 1955

Tracy, Charles, *English Gothic Choir-Stalls, 1200-1400*, Wolfeboro, New Hampshire and Woodbridge, Suffolk: Boydell Press, 1987

France
Aubert, Marcel, *La sculpture française au Moyen Âge*, Paris: Flammarion, 1946

Bridaham, Lester Burbank, *Gargoyles, chimères, and the grotesque in French Gothic sculpture*, New York: Architectural Book, 1930; 2nd edition, New York: Da Capo Press, 1969

Forsyth, William H., *The Pietà in French Late Gothic Sculpture: Regional Variations*, New York: Metropolitan Museum of Art, 1995

Mâle, Émile, *The Gothic Image: Religious Art in France of the Thirteenth Century*, New York: Harper, 1958; London: Collins, 1961 (French original, 1898)

Sauerlander, Willibald, *Gothic Sculpture in France, 1140-1270*, New York: Abrams, and London: Thames and Hudson, 1972

Germany
Liebmann, M. J., *Deutsche Plastik, 1350-1550*, Leipzig: Seemann, 1982

Italy
Pope-Hennessy, John Wyndham, *Italian Gothic Sculpture in the Victoria and Albert Museum*, New York: Phaidon, and London: Victoria and Albert Museum, 1952

Pope-Hennessy, John Wyndham, *An Introduction to Italian Sculpture. Vol. 1, Italian Gothic Sculpture*, London: Phaidon, 1955; 4th edition, 1996

PAINTING
Avril, François, *L'enluminure à l'époque gothique, 1200-1420*, Paris: Bibliothèque de l'Image, 1995

Binski, Paul, *Painters*, Toronto and Buffalo: University of Toronto Press, and London: British Museum Press, 1991

289

Brown, Sarah and David O'Connor, *Glass-painters,* Toronto: University of Toronto Press, and London: British Museum Press, 1991

Caviness, Madeline Harrison, *Paintings on Glass: Studies in Romanesque and Gothic Monumental Art*, Aldershot and Brookfield, Vermont: Variorum, 1997

De Hamel, Christopher, *Scribes and Illuminators,* Toronto and Buffalo, New York: University of Toronto Press, and London: British Museum Press, 1992

Dupont, Jacques and Cesare Gnudi, *Gothic Painting*, Geneva: Skira, 1954 (French original, 1954)

Gordon, Dillian, *The Wilton Diptych,* London: National Gallery, 1993

Schacherl, Lilliane, *Très riches heures: Behind the Gothic Masterpiece*, New York and Munich: Prestel, 1997

Scott, Kathleen L., *Later Gothic Manuscripts, 1390-1490*, London: Miller, 1996

Wieck, Roger, S., *The Book of Hours in Medieval Art and Life,* London: Sotheby, 1988

Britain
Marks, Richard, *The Golden Age of English Manuscript Painting, 1200-1400,* New York: Braziller, and London: Chatto and Windus, 1981

Morgan, Nigel J., *Early Gothic Manuscripts, 1190-1285*, New York: Oxford University Press, and London: Miller, 1982

Rickert, Margaret Josephine, *Painting in Britain: The Middle Ages,* Baltimore and Harmondsworth: Penguin, 1954; 2nd edition, 1965

Sandler, Lucy Freeman, *Gothic Manuscripts, 1285-1385,* New York: Oxford University Press, and London: Miller, 1986

France
Branner, Robert, *Manuscript Painting in Paris During the Reign of St. Louis: A Study of Styles*, Berkeley: University of California Press, 1977

Meiss, Millard, *French Painting in the Time of Jean de Berry,* New York: Braziller, 1974; London: Phaidon, 1967-69

Italy
Bomford, David et al., *Art in the Making: Italian Painting Before 1400*, London: National Gallery, 1989

Meiss, Millard, *Painting in Florence and Siena After the Black Death: The Arts, Religion and Society in the Mid-fourteenth century*, Princeton, New Jersey: Princeton University Press, 1978

APPLIED ARTS
Barnet, Peter (editor), *Images in Ivory: Precious Objects of the Gothic Age*, Detroit, Michigan: Detroit Institute of Arts, and Princeton, New Jersey: Princeton University Press, 1997

Camille, Michael, *Image on the Edge: the Margins of Medieval Art*, Cambridge, Massachusetts: Harvard University Press, and London: Reaktion, 1992

Cowen, Painton, *A Guide to Stained Glass in Britain*, London: Joseph, 1985

Goldschmidt, Ernst Philip, *Gothic and Renaissance Bookbindings: Exemplified and Illustrated from the Author's Collection*, Boston: Houghton Mifflin, and London: Benn, 1967

Grodecki, Louis and Catherine Brisac, *Gothic Stained Glass, 1200-1300*, Ithaca, New York: Cornell University Press, and London: Thames and Hudson, 1985 (French original, 1984)

Hughes, Peter, *The Wallace Collection: Catalogue of Furniture. Vol. 1, Gothic and Renaissance Style, Carved Furniture, Lacquer Furniture, Barometers and Clocks*, London: Trustees of the Wallace Collection, 1996

Kemp, Wolfgang, *The Narratives of Gothic Stained Glass*, New York and Cambridge: Cambridge University Press, 1997 (German original, 1987)

Marks, Richard, *Stained Glass in England During the Middle Ages*, Toronto and Buffalo, New York: University of Toronto Press, and London: Routledge, 1993

Souchal, Geneviève, *Masterpieces of Tapestry from the Fourteenth to the Sixteenth Century: An Exhibition at the Metropolitan Museum of Art*, New York: Metropolitan Museum of Art, 1974

MONOGRAPHS ON INDIVIDUAL ARTISTS
Cole, Bruce, *Giotto and Florentine Painting, 1280-1375*, New York: Harper and Row, 1976

Martindale, Andrew, *Simone Martini,* Oxford: Phaidon, 1988

White, John, *Duccio: Tuscan Art and the Medieval Workshop*, New York and London: Thames and Hudson, 1979

Zehnder, Frank Gunter (editor), *Stefan Lochner, Meister zu Köln: Herkunft, Werke, Wirkung*, Cologne: Verlag Locher & Wallraf-Richartz-Museum, 1993

RENAISSANCE ART

GENERAL
Aston, Margaret (editor), *The Panorama of the Renaissance*, New York: Abrams, and London: Thames and Hudson, 1996

Bia[l]ostocki, Jan, *Spätmittelalter und beginnende Neuzeit*, Berlin: Propyläen, 1972

Black, Chris et al., *Atlas of the Renaissance*, London: Cassell, 1993

Chastel, André, *The Crisis of the Renaissance, 1520-1600*, Geneva: Skira, 1968

Earls, Irene, *Renaissance Art: A Topical Dictionary*, New York: Greenwood Press, 1987

Farago, Claire (editor), *Reframing the Renaissance: Visual Culture in Europe and Latin America, 1450-1650*, New Haven, Connecticut: Yale University Press, 1995

Field, Judith Veronica and Frank A.J.L. James (editors), *Renaissance and Revolution: Humanists, Scholars, Craftsmen, and Natural Philosophers in Early Modern Europe*, New York and Cambridge: Cambridge University Press, 1993

Field, Judith Veronica, *The Invention of Infinity: Mathematics and Art in the Renaissance*, New York and Oxford: Oxford University Press, 1997

Gilbert, Creighton, *History of Renaissance Art: Painting, Sculpture, Architecture Throughout Europe*, Englewood Cliffs, New Jersey: Prentice-Hall, 1973

Gombrich, Ernst Hans, *Norm and Form: Studies in the Art of the Renaissance,* New York and London: Phaidon, 1966

Hale, John Rigby, *Artists and Warfare in the Renaissance,* New Haven, Connecticut, and London: Yale University Press, 1990

Harbison, Craig, *The Art of the Northern Renaissance*, London: Weidenfeld and Nicolson, 1995

Jardine, Lisa, *Worldly Goods,* New York: Norton, and London: Macmillan, 1996

Jestaz, Bertrand, *The Art of the Renaissance,* New York: Abrams, 1995 (French original, 1984)

Kauffmann, Georg, *Die Kunst des 16. Jahrhunderts*, Berlin: Propyläen, 1970

Kaufmann, Thomas DaCosta, *The Mastery of Nature: Aspects of Art, Science and Humanism in the Renaissance*, Princeton, New Jersey: Princeton University Press, 1993

Kemp, Martin, *The Science of Art: Optical Themes in Western Art from Brunelleschi to Seurat*, New Haven, Connecticut, and London: Yale University Press, 1989

Kraye, Jill (editor), *The Cambridge Companion to Renaissance Humanism*, New York and Cambridge: Cambridge University Press, 1996

Kristeller, Paul Oskar, *Renaissance Thought and the Arts: Collected Essays*, Princeton, New Jersey: Princeton University Press, 1990

Levey, Michael, *Early Renaissance*, Baltimore and Harmondsworth: Penguin, 1967

Levey, Michael, *High Renaissance*, Baltimore and Harmondsworth, Penguin, 1975

Osten, Gert von der, *Painting and Sculpture in Germany and the Netherlands, 1500 to 1600*, Baltimore and Harmondsworth: Penguin, 1969

Panofsky, Erwin, *Renaissance and Renascences in Western Art*, New York: Harper and Row, 1972; Stockholm: Almqvist & Wiksell, 1960, 2nd edition, 1965

Porter, Roy and Mikulás Teich (editors), *The Renaissance in National Context*, New York and Cambridge: Cambridge University Press, 1992

Snyder, James, *Northern Renaissance Art: Painting, Sculpture, the Graphic Arts From 1350 to 1575*, New York: Abrams, 1985

Strong, Roy, *Art and Power: Renaissance Festivals, 1450-1650*, Berkeley: University of California Press, and Woodbridge, Suffolk: Boydell Press, 1984

Britain

Chaney, Edward and Peter Mack (editors), *England and the Continental Renaissance: Essays in Honour of J.B. Trapp*, Rochester, New York, and Woodbridge, Suffolk: Boydell Press, 1990

Greenblatt, Stephen (editor), *Representing the English Renaissance*, Berkeley: University of California Press, 1988

Howarth, David, *Images of Rule: Art and Politics in the English Renaissance, 1485-1649*, Berkeley: University of California Press, and London: Macmillan, 1997

Italy

Ady, Cecilia Mary, *A History of Milan Under the Sforza*, New York: Putnam, and London: Methuen, 1907

Burckhardt, Jacob, *The Civilization of the Renaissance in Italy*, New York and London: Harper and Row, 1958

Burke, Peter, *Culture and Society in Renaissance Italy, 1420-1540*, New York: Scribner, and London: Batsford, 1972; revised edition as *Tradition and Innovation in Renaissance Italy: A Sociological Approach*, London: Fontana, 1974, and as *The Italian Renaissance*, Princeton, New Jersey: Princeton University Press, and Cambridge: Polity Press, 1987

Chambers, David and Jane Martineau (editors), *Splendours of the Gonzaga: Catalogue*, London: Victoria and Albert Museum, 1981

Clough, Cecil H., *Duchy of Urbino in the Renaissance*, London: Variorum, 1981

Cole, Alison, *Art of the Italian Renaissance Courts: Virtue and Magnificence*, New York: Abrams, and London: Weidenfeld and Nicolson, 1995

Hale, John Rigby (editor), *The Thames and Hudson Encyclopaedia of the Italian Renaissance*, New York and London: Thames and Hudson, 1989

Hale, John Rigby, *The Civilization of Europe in the Renaissance*, New York: Atheneum, and London: HarperCollins, 1993; 1994

Hartt, Frederick, *History of Italian Renaissance Art: Painting, Sculpture, Architecture*, London: Thames and Hudson, 1970; 4th edition, 1994

Hay, Denys, *Italy in the Age of the Renaissance 1380-1530*, New York and London: Longman, 1989

Hollingsworth, Mary, *Patronage in Renaissance Italy: From 1400 to the Early Sixteenth Century*, Baltimore: Johns Hopkins University Press, and London: Murray, 1994

Huse, Norbert and Wolfgang Wolters, *The Art of Renaissance Venice: Architecture, Sculpture and Painting, 1460-1590*, Chicago: University of Chicago Press, 1990 (German original, 1986)

Kent, Francis William, Patricia Simons with John Christopher Eade, *Patronage, Art and Society in Renaissance Italy*, New York: Oxford University Press, and Canberra: Humanities Research Centre Australia, 1987

Martineau, Jane and Charles Hope (editors), *The Genius of Venice, 1500-1600*, New York: Abrams, 1984; London: Royal Academy of Arts in association with Weidenfeld and Nicolson, 1983

Millon, Henry A. and Vittorio Magnano Lampugnani (editors), *The Renaissance from Brunelleschi to Michelangelo: The Representation of Architecture*, New York: Rizzoli, and London: Thames and Hudson, 1994 (Italian original, 1994)

Paoletti, John T., *Art in Renaissance Italy*, New York: Abrams, and London: King: 1997

Partridge, Loren W., *The Art of Renaissance Rome, 1400-1600*, New York: Abrams, and London: Calmann and King, 1996

Rosenberg, Charles M. (editor), *Art and Politics in Late Medieval and Early Renaissance Italy, 1250-1500*, Notre Dame, Indiana: University of Notre Dame Press, 1990

Rotondi, Pasquale, *The Ducal Palace of Urbino: Its Architecture and Decoration*, New York: Transatlantic Arts, and London: Tiranti, 1969 (Italian original, 1950-51)

Welch, Evelyn S., *Art and Authority in Renaissance Milan*, New Haven, Connecticut: Yale University Press, 1995

Wittkower, Rudolf, *Art and Architecture in Italy, 1600 to 1750*, Baltimore and Harmondsworth: Penguin, 1958; 3rd revised edition, 1973

Wittkower, Rudolf, *Idea and Image: Studies in the Italian Renaissance*, New York and London: Thames and Hudson, 1978

ARCHITECTURE

Argan, Giulio Carlo, *The Renaissance City*, London: Studio Vista, 1969

Hughes, Quentin and Norbert Lynton, *Renaissance Architecture*, New York: McKay, 1962

Lowry, Bates, *Renaissance Architecture*, New York: Braziller, 1962

Murray, Peter, *Renaissance Architecture*, London: Academy, 1979

Wittkower, Rudolf, *Architectural Principles in the Age of Humanism*, London: Warburg Institute, 1949; 4th edition, London: Academy, and New York: St. Martin's Press, 1988

Wölfflin, Heinrich, *Renaissance and Baroque*, Ithaca, New York: Cornell University Press, 1967

Britain

Wittkower, Rudolf, *Palladio and English Palladianism*, London: Thames and Hudson, 1974

Germany

Hitchcock, Henry Russell, *German Renaissance Architecture*, Princeton, New Jersey; Princeton University Press, 1981

291

Italy

Heydenreich, Ludwig Heinrich, *Architecture in Italy, 1400-1600. Part 1,* Harmondsworth: Penguin, 1974; as *Architecture in Italy, 1400-1500,* New Haven and London: Yale University Press, 1996

Lotz, Wolfgang, *Architecture in Italy, 1400-1600. Part 2,* Harmondsworth: Penguin, 1974; as *Architecture in Italy, 1500-1600,* New Haven and London: Yale University Press, 1995

Millon, Henry A. and Susan Scott Munshower (editors), *An Architectural Progress in the Renaissance and Baroque: Sojourns in and out of Italy,* University Park: Pennsylvania State University, 1992

Murray, Peter, *The Architecture of the Italian Renaissance,* London: Batsford, 1963

Seymour, Charles, *Sculpture in Italy, 1400 to 1500,* Harmondsworth: Penguin, 1966

SCULPTURE

Bober, Phyllis Pray and Ruth Rubinstein, *Renaissance Artists & Antique Sculpture: A Handbook of Sources,* London: Miller, and Oxford: Oxford University Press, 1986

Currie, Stuart and Peta Motture (editors), *The Sculpted Object, 1400 to 1700,* Brookfield, Vermont: Ashgate, and Aldershot: Scolar Press, 1997

Müller, Theodore, *Sculpture in the Netherlands, Germany, France and Spain, 1400-1500,* Harmondsworth: Penguin, 1966

Britain

Whinney, Margaret Dickens, *Sculpture in Britain, 1530-1830,* Baltimore and Harmondsworth: Penguin, 1964; 2nd edition, New York and London: Penguin, 1988

Germany

Pinder, Wilhelm, *Die deutsche Plastik vom ausgehenden Mittelalter bis zum Ende der Renaissance,* Berlin: Akademische Verlagsgesellschaft Athenaion, 1914-19

Italy

Avery, Charles, *Florentine Renaissance Sculpture,* New York: Harper and Row, and London: Murray, 1970

Bule, Steven, Alan Phipps Darr and Fiorella Superbi Gioffredi, *Verrocchio and Late Quattrocento Italian Sculpture,* Florence: Lettere, 1992

McHam, Sarah Blake (editor), *Looking at Italian Renaissance Sculpture,* New York and Cambridge: Cambridge University Press, 1998

Pope-Hennessy, John Wyndham, *An Introduction to Italian Sculpture. Vol. 2. Italian Renaissance Sculpture,* London: Phaidon,1958; 4th edition, 1996

Pope-Hennessy, John Wyndham, *Italian High Renaissance and Baroque Sculpture,* New York and London, Phaidon, 1958-63; 4th edition, 1996

Seymour, Charles, *Sculpture in Italy, 1400-1500,* Harmondsworth: Penguin,1966

PAINTING

Andrews, Lew, *Story and Space in Renaissance Art: the Rebirth of Continuous Narrative,* Cambridge: Cambridge University Press, 1995

Argan, Giulio Carlo, *The Renaissance,* London: Thames and Hudson, 1967

Campbell, Lorne, *Renaissance Portraits: European Portrait Painting in the 14th, 15th, and 16th Centuries,* New Haven and London: Yale University Press, 1990

Cuttler, Charles D., *Northern Painting from Pucelle to Bruegel: Fourteenth, Fifteenth and Sixteenth Centuries,* New York: Holt, 1968

Dunkerton, Jill *et al.,* *Giotto to Dürer: Early Renaissance Painting in the National Gallery,* New Haven, Connecticut: Yale University Press, and London: National Gallery, 1991

Hall, Marcia B., *Color and Meaning: Practice and Theory in Renaissance Painting,* Cambridge: Cambridge University Press, 1992

Humfrey, Peter and Martin Kemp (editors), *The Altarpiece in the Renaissance,* Cambridge: Cambridge University Press, 1990

White, John, *The Birth and Rebirth of Pictorial Space,* New York: Yoseloff, 1958; London: Faber, 1957, 3rd edition, Faber, 1987

France

Ring, Grete, *A Century of French Painting, 1400-1500,* London: Phaidon, 1949

Laborde, Léon, *La renaissance des arts à la cour de France,* Paris: Potier, 1850-53

Italy

Alexander, Jonathan James Graham, *Italian Renaissance Illuminations,* New York: Braziller, and London: Chatto and Windus, 1977

Alexander, Jonathan James Graham (editor), *The Painted Page: Italian Renaissance Book Illumination, 1450-1550,* New York and Munich: Prestel, 1994

Antal, Frederick, *Florentine Painting and Its Social Background: The Bourgeois Republic Before Cosimo Medici's Advent to Power, XIV and Early XV Centuries,* London: Kegan Paul, 1948

Baxandall, Michael, *Painting and Experience in Fifteenth Century Italy: A Primer in the Social History of Pictorial Style,* Oxford: Clarendon Press, 1942

Baxandall, Michael, *Giotto and the Orators: Humanist Observers of Painting in Italy and the Discovery of Pictorial Composition, 1350-1450,* Oxford: Clarendon Press, 1971

Borsook, Eve, *The Mural Painters of Tuscany: From Cimabue to Andrea del Sarto,* New York and London: Phaidon, 1960; 2nd edition, New York: Oxford University Press, and Oxford: Clarendon Press, 1980

Evans, Mark L., *The Sforza Hours,* New York: New Amsterdam Books, and London: British Library, 1992

Freedberg, S.J., *Painting of the High Renaissance in Rome and Florence,* Cambridge, Massachusetts: Harvard University Press,1961

Gundersheimer, Werner W., *Ferrara: the Style of a Renaissance Despotism,* Princeton, New Jersey: Princeton University Press, 1973

Labella, Vincenzo, *A Season of Giants: Michelangelo, Leonardo, Raphael, 1492-1508,* Boston and London: Little Brown, 1990

Marle, Raimond van, *The Development of the Italian Schools of Painting,* The Hague: Nijhoff, 1923-28

Salmi, Mario, *Italian Miniatures,* New York: Abrams, 1954; 2nd edition, New York: Abrams, 1956; London: Collins, 1957

Netherlands

Friedländer, Max J., *Early Netherlandish Painting,* Leiden: Sitjhoff, 1967-76 (Dutch original, 1924-37)

Pächt, Otto, *Early Netherlandish Painting: From Rogier van der Weyden to Gerard David,* London: Miller, 1997 (German original, 1994)

Panofsky, Erwin, *Early Netherlandish Painting: Its Origins and Character,* Cambridge, Massachusetts: Harvard University Press, 1953

Whinney, Margaret Dickens, *Early Flemish Painting,* New York: Praeger, and London: Faber, 1968

MONOGRAPHS ON INDIVIDUAL ARTISTS

Avery, Charles, *Donatello: An Introduction,* New York: Icon, 1994

Beck, James H., *Jacopo della Quercia,* New York: Columbia University Press, 1991

Berti, Luciano, *Masaccio,* University Park: Pennsylvania State University Press, 1967 (Italian original, 1954)

Boucher, Bruce, *Andrea Palladio: The Architect in His time,* New York and London: Abbeville, 1994

Butterfield, Andrew, *The Sculptures of Andrea del Verrocchio,* New York and London: Yale University Press, 1997

Calvesi, Maurizio, *Piero della Francesca,* New York: Rizzoli, 1998

Goldscheider, Ludwig, *Ghiberti,* London: Phaidon, 1949

Greenhalgh, Michael, *Donatello and His Sources,* New York: Holmes and Meier, 1982

Holberton, Paul, *Palladio's Villas: Life in the Renaissance Countryside,* London: Murray, 1990

Kemp, Martin, *Leonardo da Vinci: The Marvellous Works of Nature and Man,* Cambridge, Massachusetts: Harvard University Press, and London: Dent, 1981

Lavin, Marilyn Aronberg, *Piero della Francesca and His Legacy,* Washington, D.C.: National Gallery of Art, 1995

Lightbown, Ronald, *Sandro Botticelli: Life and Work,* London: Thames and Hudson, 1989

Pächt, Otto, *Van Eyck and the Founders of Early Netherlandish Painting,* London: Miller, 1994 (German original, 1989)

Partridge, Loren W., Fabrizio Mancinelli and Gianluigi Colalucci, *Michelangelo — the Last Judgement: a Glorious Restoration,* New York: Abrams, 1997

Poeschke, Joachim, *Donatello and His World: Sculptors of the Italian Renaissance,* New York: Abrams, 1993 (German original, 1990)

Poeschke, Joachim, *Michelangelo and His World: Sculpture of the Italian Renaisssance,* New York: Abrams, 1996 (German original)

Pope-Hennessy, John Wyndham, *Donatello: Sculptor,* New York and London: Abbeville, 1993

Reti, Ladislao, *The Unknown Leonardo,* New York: McGraw-Hill, and London: Hutchinson, 1974

Saalman, Howard, *Filippo Brunelleschi: The Buildings,* London: Zwemmer, 1993

Spike, John T., *Fra Angelico,* New York and London: Abbeville, 1996

Spike, John T., *Masaccio,* New York and London: Abbeville, 1995

Tavernor, Robert, *Palladio and Palladianism,* London: Thames and Hudson, 1991

Tavenor, Robert, *On Alberti and the Art of Building,* New Haven, Connecticut and London: Yale University Press, 1998

BAROQUE ART

GENERAL

Anderson, Liselotte, *Baroque and Rococo Art,* New York and London: Abrams, 1969

Battisti, Eugenio, *Rinascimento e barocco,* Turin: Einaudi, 1960

Bazin, Germain, *Baroque and Rococo,* London: Thames and Hudson, 1964

Bazin, Germain, *The Baroque: Principles, Styles, Modes, Themes,* London: Thames and Hudson, 1968

Downes, Kerry, entry on Baroque in *Dictionary of Art. Vol. 3,* London: Macmillan, 1996

Friedrich, Carl Joachim, *The Age of the Baroque, 1610-1660,* New York: Harper, 1952

Golzio, Vincenzo, *Seicento e settecento,* Turin: Unione tipografico-editrice torinese, 3rd edition, 1968

Griseri, Andreina, *Le metamorfosi del barocco,* Turin: Einaudi, 1967

Held, Julius Samuel and Donald Posner, *Seventeenth and Eighteenth Century Art: Baroque Painting, Sculpture, Architecture,* New York: Abrams, 1972

Hempel, Eberhard, *Baroque Art and Architecture in Central Europe: Germany, Austria, Switzerland, Hungary, Poland,* Harmondsworth: Penguin,1965

Hubala, Erich, *Baroque and Rococo,* London: Herbert, 1989

Keleman, Pál, *Baroque and Rococo in Latin America,* New York: Macmillan, 1951

Keller, Harald, *Die Kunst des 18. Jahrhunderts,* Berlin: Propyläen, 1971

Kitson, Michael, *The Age of Baroque,* London: Hamlyn , 1967

Martin, John Rupert, *Baroque,* London: Lane, 1977

Pevsner, Nikolaus, *Studies in Art, Architecture and Design. Vol. 1, from Mannerism to Romanticism,* London: Thames and Hudson, 1968

Pigler, Andor, *Barockthemen: eine Auswahl von Verzeichnissen zur Ikonographie des 17. und 18. Jahrhunderts,* Budapest: Verlag der Ungarischen Akademie der Wissenschaften, 1956; 2nd edition, Budapest: Akadémiai Kiadó, 1974

Sewter, A.C., *Baroque and Rococo Art,* London: Thames and Hudson, 1972

Tapié, Victor Lucien, *The Age of Grandeur: Baroque and Classicism in Europe,* New York: Grove Press,1960; 2nd edition as *The Age of Grandeur: Baroque Art and Architecture,* New York: Praeger, 1966 (French original, 1957)

Webb, G F, "Baroque Art," *Proceedings of the British Academy,* 33 (1947): 131 (1948)

Weisbach, Werner, *Der Barock als Kunst der Gegenreformation,* Berlin: Cassirer,1921

Weisbach, Werner, *Die Kunst des Barock in Italien, Frankreich, Deutschland und Spanien,* Berlin: Propyläen, 1924

Wölfflin, Heinrich, *Renaissance and Baroque,* Ithaca, New York: Cornell University Press, 1967

Germany

Biermann, Georg, *Deutsches Barock und Rococo,* Leipzig: Schwabach, 1914

Italy

Haskell, Francis, *Patrons and Painters: a Study of the Relations Between Italian Art and Society in the Age of the Baroque,* London: Chatto and Windus, and New York: Knopf, 1963; revised and enlarged edition, New Haven: Yale University Press,1980

Lees-Milne, James, *Baroque in Italy,* London: Batsford, 1959

Wittkower, Rudolf, *Art and Architecture in Italy, 1600-1750,* Harmondsworth: Penguin, 1958; 3rd revised ediiton, 1973

Portugal

Lees-Milne, James, *Baroque in Spain and Portugal and Its Antecedents,* London: Batsford, 1960

Spain

Lees-Milne, James, *Baroque in Spain and Portugal and Its Antecedents,* London: Batsford, 1960

Weisbach, Werner, *Spanish Baroque Art: Three Lectures,* Cambridge: Cambridge University Press, 1941

ARCHITECTURE

Blunt, Anthony, *Baroque and Rococo Architecture and Decoration,* London: Elek, 1978

Bourke, John, *Baroque Churches of Central Europe*, London: Faber, 1958; 2nd edition, 1962

Brinckmann, Albert Erich, *Die Baukunst des 17. und 18. Jahrhunderts*, Berlin: Akademische Verlagsgesellschaft Athenaion, 1915-19

Kaufmann, Emil, *Architecture in the Age of reason: Baroque and Post-Baroque in England, Italy and France*, Cambridge, Massachusetts: Harvard University Press,1955

Austria
Powell, Nicolas, *From Baroque to Rococo: An Introduction to German and Austrian Architecture from 1580 to 1790*, New York: Praeger, and London: Faber, 1959

Britain
Downes, Kerry, *English Baroque Architecture*, London: Zwemmer, 1966

Germany
Powell, Nicolas, *From Baroque to Rococo: an Introduction to German and Austrian Architecture From 1580 to 1790*, London: Faber, and New York: Praeger,1959

Italy
Millon, Henry A. and Susan Scott Munshower (editors), *An Architectural Progress in the Renaissance and Baroque: Sojourns In and Out of Italy*, University Park: Pennsylvania State University, 1992

SCULPTURE
Avery, Charles, *Studies in European Sculpture. II*, London: Christie's, 1988

Brinckmann, Albert Erich, *Barockskulptur: Entwicklungsgeschichte der Skulptur in den romanischen und germanischen Ländern seit Michelangelo bis zum 18. Jahrhunderts*, Potsdam: Akademische Verlagsgesellschaft Athenaion, 1917; 3rd edition, 1932

Busch, Harald and Bernd Lohse (editors), *Baroque Sculpture*, New York: Macmillan, and London: Batsford, 1964

Currie, Stuart and Peta Motture (editors), *The Sculpted Object, 1400 to 1700*, Brookfield, Vermont: Ashgate, and Aldershot: Scolar Press, 1997

Fagiolo dell'Arco, Maurizio, *Great Baroque and Rococo Sculpture*, New York: Reynal, 1978 (Italian original)

Novotny, Fritz, *Painting and Sculpture in Europe, 1780 to 1880*, Harmondsworh: Penguin, 1960

Germany
Sitwell, Sacheverell, *German Baroque Sculpture*, London: Duckworth, 1938

Italy
Enggass, Robert, *Early Eighteenth-Century Sculpture in Rome: An Illustrated Catalogue Raisonné*, University Park: Pennsylvania State University Press, 1976

Kirwin, W. Chandler, *Powers Matchless: the Pontificate of Urban VIII, the Baldachin and Gian Lorenzo Bernini*, New York: Lang, 1997

Montagu, Jennifer, *Roman Baroque Sculpture: The Industry of Art*, New Haven, Connecticut: Yale University Press, 1989

Montagu, Jennifer, *Gold, Silver, and Bronze: Metal Sculpture of the Roman Baroque*, Princeton, New Jersey: Princeton University Press, 1996

Pope-Hennessy, John Wyndham, *Italian High Renaissance and Baroque Sculpture*, New York and London: Phaidon, 1958-63; 4th edition, 1996

Ricci, Corrado, *Baroque Architecture and Sculpture in Italy*, London: Heinemann, 1912

Netherlands
Lawrence, Cynthia Miller, *Flemish Baroque Commemorative Monuments, 1566-1725*, New York: Garland, 1981

Spain
Pillement, Georges, *La sculpture baroque espagnole*, Paris: Michel, 1945

Painting
Baroque Painting, Hauppauge, New York: Barron, 1998

Minty, Nancy, *In the Eye of the Beholder: Northern Baroque Paintings from the Collection of Henry H. Weldon*, New Orleans: New Orleans Museum of Art, 1997

Pevsner, Nikolaus and Otto Grautoff, *Barockmalerei in den romanischen Ländern*, Potsdam: Akademische Verlagsgesellschaft Athenaion, 1928

Prater, Andreas and Herman Bauer, *Painting of the Baroque*, New York and Cologne: Taschen, 1997

France
Weisbach, Werner, *Französische Malerei des VII. Jahrhunderts: im Rahmen von Kultur und Gesellschaft*, Berlin: Keller, 1932

Germany
Tintelnot, Hans, *Die barocke Frescomalerei in Deutschland: ihre Entwicklung und europäische Wirkung*, Munich: Bruckmann, 1951

Italy
Briganti, Giuliano, *Pietro da Cortona, o, Della pittura barocca*, Florence: Sansoni, 1962; 2nd edition, 1982

Finaldi, Gabriele and Michael Kitson, *Discovering the Italian Baroque: The Denis Mahon Collection*, London: National Gallery, 1997

McComb, Arthur Kilgore, *The Baroque Painters of Italy*, Cambridge, Massachusetts: Harvard University Press, 1934

McCorquodale, Charles, *The Baroque Painters of Italy*, Oxford: Phaidon, 1979

Voss, Hermann, *Baroque Painting in Rome*, San Francisco: Wofsy Fine Arts, 1997 (German original, 1925)

Netherlands
Sutton, Peter S., *The Age of Rubens*, Boston: Museum of Fine Arts, 1993

MONOGRAPHS ON INDIVIDUAL ARTISTS
Alpers, Svetlana, *The Making of Rubens*, New Haven and London: Yale University Press, 1995

Beard, Geoffrey W., *The Work of Christopher Wren*, London: Bloomsbury, 1987

Belkin, Kristin Lohse, *Rubens*, London: Phaidon, 1998

Blunt, Anthony, *Borromini*, London: Lane, 1979

Bordier, Cyril, *Louis le Vau: architecte*, Paris: Éditions Léonce Laget, 1998

Braham, Alan and Peter Smith, *François Mansart*, London: Zwemmer, 1973

Brown, Jonathan and Carmen Garrido, *Velázquez: The Technique of Genius*, New Haven and London: Yale University Press, 1998

Clark, Kenneth, *An Introduction to Rembrandt*, London: Murray, 1978

Coope, Rosalys, *Salomon de Brosse and the Development of the Classical Style in French Architecture from 1565 to 1630*, London: Zwemmer, 1972

Downes, Kerry, *The Architecture of Wren*, New York: Universe, and London: Granada, 1982

Friedländer, Max J., *Pieter Brueghel*, Leiden: Sitjhoff, 1976

Grimm, Claus, *Frans Hals: The Complete Work*, New York: Abrams, 1990 (German original, 1989)

Grimschitz, Bruno, *Johann Lucas von Hildebrandt*, Vienna: Herold, 1959

Hauer, Christian E. (editor), *Christopher Wren and the Many Sides of Genius: Proceedings of a Christopher Wren Symposium*, Lewiston, Maine: Mellen, 1997

Jong, Jan de *et al.*, *Pieter Bruegel*, Zwolle: Waanders, 1997

Langdon, Helen, *Caravaggio: A Life*, London: Chatto and Windus, 1998

Lo Bianco, Anna (editor), *Pietro da Cortona, 1597-1669*, Milan: Electa: 1997

Marder, Tod A., *Bernini and the Art of Architecture*, New York: Abbeville, 1998

Moreno Mendoza, Arsenio, *Zurbarán*, Madrid: Electa, 1998

Raspe, Martin, *Die Architektursystem Borrominis*, Munich: Deutscher Kunstverlag, 1994

Reuther, Hans, *Balthasar Neumann, der Mainfränkische Barockbaumeister*, Munich: Suddeutscher Verlag, 1983

Rodríguez G. de Ceballos, Alfonso, *Los Churriguera*, Madrid: Instituto Diego Velázquez del Consejo Superior de Investigaciones Científicas, 1971

Schneider, Gerd, *Guarino Guarini: ungebauten Bauten*, Wiesbaden: Reichert, 1997

Wheelock, Arthur K. *et al.*, *Anthony van Dyck*, New York: Abrams, 1990

White, Christopher, *Rembrandt by Himself*, New Haven, Connecticut, and London: Yale University Press, 1999

Wied, Alexander, *Bruegel*, Paris: Gallimard, 1997

Wilson-Smith, Timothy, *Caravaggio*, London: Phaidon, 1998

Wittkower, Rudolf, *Bernini: The Sculptor of the Roman Baroque*, London: Phaidon, 1955; revised edition, Milan: Electa, 1990

INDEX

Works ascribed to a specific artist or architect are indexed under the person's name, shown in CAPITAL letters. Unascribed works are indexed by title of work and/or by location of the work. *See* references are provided to assist in finding the correct name or location (e.g., *Bacchus and Ariadne. See* TITIAN). For illustration references, the reader is directed to the caption of the illustration. Illustration page numbers end with an italicized *c* (e.g., Abbot Guido, 43*c*). Page numbers ending with (bar) refer to the sidebar of a page (e.g., Areopagiticus, Dionysius, 99(bar)). Page numbers ending with an italicized *g* refer to words in the glossary (e.g., Altarpiece, definition of, 283*g*).